Engine Whistles

By MABEL O'DONNELL

Illustrated by

Florence and Margaret Hoopes

The Alice and Jerry Basic Reading Program

ROW, PETERSON AND COMPANY

Evanston, Illinois   White Plains, New York

Contents

TOWN IN THE VALLEY — 1879

CITY ON THE HILL — 1910

TODAY — AND THEN TOMORROW

5151

TOWN in the VALLEY
1879

"Puffing Billy"

It was a summer's day late in the 1870's. High in the southern sky the hot noonday sun blazed down upon ripening grainfields and far-reaching stretches of unbroken prairie. Not a breeze rippled the prairie grasses! Not a birdcall broke the hot, dead stillness in which ears attuned to listening might have heard the corn grow.

Suddenly, out of the heat and the stillness, came the sharp, unexpected sound of an engine whistle; and round a curve from the eastward

5

came a little wood-burning engine. Soot and sparks and cinders rained from the smokestack in spite of the net, or "cinder catcher," which covered its top. From the engine boiler came the s-s-s-s sound of escaping steam. With a steady beat of iron wheels on iron rails, the four pony wheels and the pair of big driving wheels followed the rails which led to the westward.

Out from the window at the right of the cab, looking too big and powerful for the engine which carried him, leaned Bill Turner, the engineer. The hot breeze from the hurrying engine blew through his thick brown hair. His blue shirt, wide open at the throat, was wet with sweat. Great drops of sweat raced with one another and made white, wavy tracks down his soot-blackened face and neck and arms.

There was an amused twinkle in Bill's eye as he watched the track ahead. An amused twinkle in his eye, but a queer downward turn at the corner of his mouth! Could it be that he was ashamed to be caught driving this "teakettle" engine?

"Here I am," he broke forth at last in a deep-throated chuckle. "Big Bill Turner, crack engineer of the *Prairie Flyer*, bringing this 'puffing billy' home to roost!"

"'Puffing billy'! Don't call her that! That isn't the name of this engine! You know it isn't! It's the *Pioneer!* Isn't her name painted right on the side of the engine cab! In gold letters, too!"

With this burst of indignation a thin, long-legged, sandy-haired boy jumped down from a high stool in the center of the engine cab. He was dressed in short, tight trousers, long, black stockings, and high, buttoned shoes. His white blouse was pulled in at the waist with a draw-string. Sitting on top of his head was a little round straw hat with a ribbon hanging down the back. What in the world was he doing in an engine cab, dressed in clothes like that?

"*Pioneer* may be her name, lad, but a 'puffing billy' she is!" chuckled Engineer Bill. "'Puffing billies' they all are to a railroad man, every wood-burning engine of them all. 'Puffing billies' they've been since the first of their kind came out of England."

BOYS' CLOTHES

"'Puffing billy'! What a name!" replied the boy in disgust. "That's worse even than 'choo-choo'! Of course, I figured out long ago why engines are called 'choo-choos'! That's the noise the steam makes when it escapes through the smokestack. I suppose they're 'puffing billies' because they puff smoke and cinders from their smokestacks, too. Or maybe because they puff so when they're pulling heavy loads. Anyway, I can't see anything funny in that name."

"Easy, lad," grinned Engineer Bill. "You've a soft spot in your heart for engines, that's plain to be seen. And you don't want people to be calling them names! It's hard to tell where names come from; but once they're here, they have a way of sticking. I've noticed that."

"Why couldn't it have been an American who invented the steam engine? Why couldn't it?" the boy went on.

"Because all the smart men aren't on this side of the Atlantic," replied Engineer Bill, with a shake of his big head. "I hate to admit it, but that man Stephenson was smarter than we were that time."

"Anyway, I know something that didn't come out of England," the boy hurried on. "That's the

cowcatcher! My father told me about that. You
see, there were plenty of hedges and fences in
England to keep the cows away from the tracks.
But over here we didn't have any fences when we
started to build railroads. Hardly any! So we
put a cowcatcher on the front of the first engine

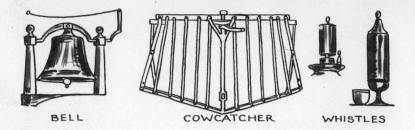

BELL   COWCATCHER   WHISTLES

that came over — to push the cows out of the way. I think that was a very smart idea."

"Smart or not, we've been ready and waiting for those cows ever since," came the laughing voice of Pierre, the wiry, dark-haired, dark-eyed fireman, from his place at the left of the engine cab. "I've never seen an engine without a cow-catcher, that's certain."

Even as Pierre was talking, Engineer Bill's hand was on the whistle cord. Two long, two short and deafening blasts sounded above the steady beat of the iron wheels.

"Two long, two short! That means we're coming to a crossroad!" shouted the boy, turning and twisting in his efforts to see around Fireman Pierre and out of the window of the cab.

Once again came the warning blast! There ahead of the engine was the crossroad. There on the crossroad, not ten feet from the track, a horse hitched to a light, two-seated spring wagon reared with its forelegs in the air. At one minute it seemed certain that the horse would dash against the oncoming train, at the next that it would turn and race wildly away. The driver was standing up in his excitement, handling the reins and calling to the frightened horse. The woman at his side clung wildly to the seat with one hand and with the other covered her face from the terrible things about to happen. As the train rolled by, the men had a glimpse of children climbing to safety over the rear end of the spring wagon.

"Cowcatcher!" thundered Engineer Bill. "It's a horse catcher an engine needs! There's one of those good-for-nothing critters kicking up its heels at every crossroad! Can't get used to the sound of a good engine, not if it lives to be a hundred! If you like engines, boy, you'll have to hate horses. The two things just don't go together."

"Hum-m-m-m," said Pierre with a long-drawn-out sigh, as he ran his hand across his forehead and snapped off the drops of sweat. "We didn't need a close call like that to make us hotter on a day like this." Then he opened wide the door of the firebox and reached into the tender behind him for more wood.

"I'll help!" cried the boy, turning eagerly around and making a grab for the woodpile.

"You'll stay where you are, Mr. Thomas Hastings, and you'll keep your hands to yourself," thundered the big voice of Engineer Bill. "If your father didn't own a good share of this railroad, you'd never be riding in this engine cab. I'm not supposed to allow it, and he knows it. If you like engines so well that he can't say no to you, what can I do about it? But see to it that you keep your hands to yourself."

"Don't let him fool you, lad," grinned Pierre, as the logs flew into the firebox. "In spite of his crabbing, he'd do a lot himself for a boy who likes engines. But he's right! Keep your hands to yourself, and you'll live to bring this 'puffing billy' safely home. We can't let anything happen to keep you from riding at the throttle of the *Pioneer* in the Fourth-of-July parade tomorrow."

"Fourth of July! I almost forgot! I told you we should have a flag, lots of them, even if it is the day before," insisted Tom. Then, as a fresh burst of soot and sparks and cinders rained from the smokestack, he stopped talking and covered his face with his hands for protection.

Steam hissed from the safety valve, and long lines of black smoke and white steam trailed back over the wooden coaches which rocked along the

track and followed the tender. Big Bill's hand
opened wide the throttle, and the glint in his eye
turned to a look of pleased satisfaction.

"You can still do more than twenty, my daisy," he said softly, as if he were conscious of no one else in the world but himself and the engine. "Twenty-five years ago, when I was fireman on your first run, you couldn't do much more than that, not without bursting your boiler. Wait until Old Joe hears about this! They wanted to bring you home on a flatcar — the mayor, the banker, and the rest of the Big Ones! It took Big Bill to tell them! Home, yes, home under your own steam! That's how you'd come! Home in time for the parade and not on a flatcar, either! Wonder what they're thinking about us now back there in those rocking coaches? Wonder what they're saying now when we're throwing cinders in their eyes?"

Once more Big Bill's hand was on the whistle cord. One long blast and then another! From the window of the cab Tom could see a river making a sweeping curve in their direction.

"I know! That's for the bridgetender, that whistle," he shouted to Pierre.

Sure enough! Engineer Bill released the throttle, the train slowed down, and almost at once the engine and the coaches were slipping out over the trestles and the wooden sleepers of a railroad bridge. There in his watchman's cabin, halfway across the bridge, the watchman was waving his cane from the doorway. Waving his cane with one hand and with the other holding his big straw hat on top of the red bandana which protected his head from the heat!

"Don't fall in the river, you hothead!" teased Pierre, as the train slipped by.

"Can't the railroad find you an engine? Keep up the steam in that boiler! Don't let that tea-kettle stop on my bridge!" scoffed the bridge-tender in return.

"Now he'll start walking the sleepers!" cried Tom, peering as far back as he could along the tracks. "There've been enough sparks from this engine to start half a dozen fires. But he'll put them out. That's his job! He can walk the sleepers fast, too. I walked them once on the railroad bridge back home — away across the Big Turtle River. But not fast! You don't walk fast the first time — not if you've got sense."

No sooner had the *Pioneer* reached the western end of the bridge than another idea popped into Tom's head.

"Why did the railroad put the watchman's cabin in the middle of the bridge?" he questioned Engineer Bill.

"That's where it belongs," chuckled Engineer Bill. "It keeps the bridgetender's eyes open and his mind on his job. If he goes to sleep and lets the bridge burn down, a good-for-nothing bridgetender will go down, too. Then, if he wants dry land, he can swim for it."

"Oh, I see! I might have thought of that myself," said Tom with a thoughtful look, as if he were turning things over and over in his mind and seeing how they all fitted together. "Might not be so much fun being a bridgetender! Kind of lonesome, don't you think?"

Neither Bill nor Pierre answered. For a time no more was said. Big Bill's eyes were glued on the track ahead. Pierre still fed the hungry mouth of the firebox. Steam hissed and cinders flew, and Tom looked out above and below Big Bill's sooty arms.

Objects first seen as faraway specks on the horizon came closer and ever closer, only to disappear into the widening distance behind them.

Fields of yellowing grain slipped swiftly by. Now
a brook with bending willows! Here a hillside and
a patch of woods and sheep grazing in sunny pas-
tures! Gray, unpainted houses and red barns,
lonely-looking among the fields of corn grown
knee-high by the Fourth of July!

17

All this Big Bill saw from the corner of his eye. All this while the sturdy little wood-burning engine puffed its way to the westward!

"It's a great country, lad," said Engineer Bill at last, without a turn of his head in Tom's direction. "A great country! But it needs more than rich soil to make it prosper. Twenty-five years ago tomorrow, on the Fourth of July, your grandfather drove the first spike in the first tie on this railroad. Do you know what that spike did?"

"What?" asked Tom eagerly. "What did it do?"

"It kept Hastings Mills from becoming a sleepy, no-account little village and changed it into a lively, up-and-coming railroad town. You see, that's what we called the town in those days, not Hastings, but Hastings Mills.

"Way off yonder," Engineer Bill continued, nodding his head to either side, "farther than you can see, are many other towns that started and stopped and got nowhere. Got nowhere why? Because there wasn't someone like your grandfather with sense enough to bring a railroad to their door. No way to send their grain to market! No way to ship their cattle! Mark my words, lad! It takes a railroad to make a town."

"Hastings has had a railroad for twenty-five years, and there are almost twelve thousand people living there now! That proves it! That proves what you say!" Tom burst forth. "No wonder we're having a celebration! No wonder everyone insisted on bringing home the first engine to ride in the parade. It's been sitting long enough in the roundhouse at the other end of the line. It's time it came home to roost. That's what Grandfather says."

"He can say what he likes, but 'puffing billy' will never make the home roost if we don't reach tank town soon," Pierre broke in, with a worried glance at the fast-disappearing woodpile.

Big Bill glanced back at the tender with a look of alarm in his own eye. "It takes more to make you puff than it did in your young days," he said, as if talking to the engine. Then to Pierre he added, "Keep her steam up! We'll make it yet!" Then his hand opened wide the throttle.

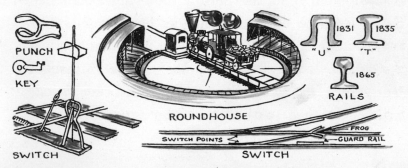

PUNCH
KEY
RAILS
SWITCH
ROUNDHOUSE
SWITCH
SWITCH POINTS
FROG
GUARD RAIL

"Tank Town"

Time went by. Tom, with his eye on the wood-pile, began to count the disappearing logs. Twenty, nineteen, eighteen, seventeen! At this rate the steam would begin to go down at any minute. Sixteen, fifteen, fourteen — at last! Round a bend in the track a wooden water tank came into view, standing high in the air on its great wooden legs. It was alone on the prairie except for the two or three houses which huddled at its foot.

So this was "tank town." Tom remembered stopping here last night. He had been riding in a coach then with his father and grandfather, traveling to the other end of the line to bring home the *Pioneer*. It had been black night with no moon, no stars, when the train stopped. The kerosene lamps in the coaches and the kerosene headlight on the engine hadn't been much good to see by. But now he could see! Now he could see everything!

One long blast of the train whistle and Engineer Bill released the throttle. The train slowed almost to a stop. The brakeman, leaping from the steps of the first coach, ran forward in front of the engine. Switch key in hand, he opened the switch and allowed the *Pioneer* to slip into the siding.

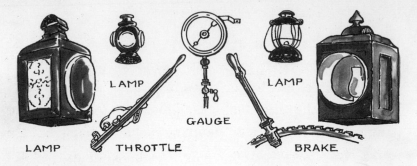

LAMP   LAMP   GAUGE   LAMP

LAMP   THROTTLE   BRAKE

"Look! He slipped! He almost fell!" cried Tom in excited alarm. "He might have rolled under the engine! Now he's up! Now he's all right!"

"Thank fortune!" boomed the big voice of Engineer Bill, as the sweat drops raced faster and faster down his soot-blackened face. "We've had enough for one day. There's many a fine lad who has lost his life under the wheels while throwing switches. Many another's been caught between cars or has lost his fingers coupling cars together. If you're set on being a railroad man, son, there's plenty still to be done to make railroads safe for the men who are running them."

Now with one crash and then another as the couplings slacked between the cars, "puffing billy" came to a stop on a siding beside the water tank. At once Engineer Bill was down from the cab, an oilcan with a very long spout in his hand. Down went the oil into every place on the engine where oil should go. By this time the wheel tapper from "tank town" was going from one coach wheel to another, tapping with his hammer and listening for possible cracks or breaks.

Before Big Bill had one foot from the cab, the man in charge of the water tank had pulled a rope and had turned the long, swinging spout which extended out from the side of the tank. The nose of the spout fitted right into an opening in the side of the smaller water tank at the back of the engine tender. Tom, jumping from the cab, stood listening to the gush of the water. He followed with his eye the long pipe which led from the tender tank to the engine boiler. "Huh! That's how water gets to the boiler," he thought to himself. "Huh! That's easy!"

Another minute and everyone in "tank town" was crowded round the engine. Remarks flew thick and fast.

"Twenty-five years and still going! Pretty good for a teakettle engine! Take a look at that smokestack and the size of those driving wheels! Not

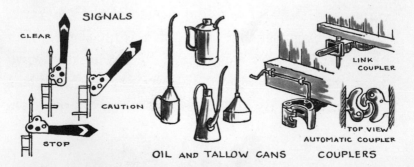

SIGNALS
CLEAR
CAUTION
STOP
OIL AND TALLOW CANS
LINK COUPLER
TOP VIEW
AUTOMATIC COUPLER
COUPLERS

much like the *Prairie Flyer!* The train crew that stopped here yesterday said something about a parade. Don't tell us the mayor and the president of the railroad are riding behind this 'puffing billy'!"

Perhaps it was just as well that Tom was busy by this time and was not around to hear all these remarks. Over at the edge of the track near the water tank were the coalbins, and today in one of the bins was a load of wood for the *Pioneer*. With never a thought for his fine clothes, Tom set to work with a will.

"This load will carry us clear to Hastings, won't it?" he asked Pierre, as log followed log into the front of the engine tender. "It's a hot day for work like this. It might be fun if someone would turn the waterspout on us. How would you like that?"

"It would suit me to a T," grinned Pierre. "I couldn't be wetter than I am now. If you call this hard work, you should have been here in the days when we had to haul water in buckets from the river to fill the tanks. I tell you, those were the days! Why, we thought we were in luck when we finally got a hose to reach from the river to the tender and a pump to pump the water."

"It was a smart idea, wasn't it," said Tom, "to dig a well by the side of the track and then build a storage tank like this one to hold the water? I wonder who thought of that. I suppose someday someone will have an even better idea."

"Talk sense! How could he? What could be better than a storage tank?" said Pierre, as if that ended the matter. Then suddenly he glanced up, only to exclaim in astonishment,

"My stars! Here come the owners of the railroad! Wait until your father sets his eyes on you!"

Sure enough! Out from the door of one of the passenger coaches and down the track toward the engine came a group of important-looking men. There were tall men and short men among them, and fat men and thin, but all of them were very important looking. Some wore derby hats, and some carried canes. Two among the number wore high silk hats, and they were the most important looking of all.

"Whew-w-w!" chuckled Pierre, under his breath. "The mayor and the president! They put on their high hats to ride on 'puffing billy'!"

By this time the first man in the group had reached the woodpile. Something about his smile, his blue eyes, and the expression on his face made him look strangely like Tom.

"Hello, Pierre! Hello, Tom!" he called with an amused smile, as he took Tom by the shoulder and turned him around to look him over. "Good gracious, boy! Wait until your mother sees you!

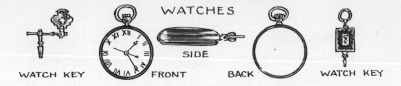

WATCHES

WATCH KEY   FRONT   SIDE   BACK   WATCH KEY

How are you behaving yourself in that engine cab? Come here a minute! I want you to meet Mr. Gates, the President of the Hastings, Lake Shore, and Western Railroad."

Tom doffed his hat, left the woodpile, and walked in Mr. Gates's direction.

"My grandson, sir," said the man who had been talking to Tom, "and you can see for yourself he's learning all there is to know about railroading from the ground up."

Now, if Tom was hot and dirty, so was the president. But it's quite unusual for a man to be tall and important looking and hot and dirty at the same time. That's why it was so amusing to watch the president wipe his face with his big white handkerchief. Everywhere he wiped, he left a long, black soot streak.

Tom was sure that he would burst out laughing if he kept looking at the streaks. So he shook hands and said, "How do you do," and fixed his eyes on Mr. Gates's watch chain. The chain reached right across the front of Mr. Gates from one vest pocket to another. There were half a

dozen gold charms hanging down from it. They
showed how important Mr. Gates really was.

Tom knew all about that watch chain. The
reason was that right across the front of his grandfather was another chain just like it. Once, when
Tom's Aunt Sally had been a little girl, she had
been very sick, so sick that she had had to have
her two long braids cut off. Grandfather had had

Aunt Sally's hair made into a watch chain. Now Tom wondered who had been sick in Mr. Gates's family. Just then Mr. Gates pulled his watch from his pocket. Tom wasn't surprised at that, either. He had seen lots of gold watches just like that. You had to open the hinged cover before you could see the face. You wound it with a key, just as you would a clock. The watch was as big as a turnip.

Suddenly Tom realized that Mr. Gates was speaking to him. "So you are Thomas Hastings, the Third," he was saying, smiling pleasantly down at Tom. "I'm certainly glad to meet you. What do you think you're going to be when you grow up — the Mayor of Hastings like your grandfather, a banker like your father, or a railroad president like me?"

"I'm going to be an engineer like Big Bill Turner," said Tom with conviction, "or else I'm going to build engines. I don't know which."

Tom couldn't understand why Mr. Gates looked so amused. There wasn't anything funny in what Tom had said. Tom's face turned red with embarrassment. It took his grandfather to save the day.

"I told you the railroad was in his blood, Gates," said Mayor Hastings. "But never you mind, lad," he added, turning to Tom. "Keep right on thinking! A good engineer is nothing to be ashamed of. Neither is a good railroad mechanic! Be one or the other and be a good one, and we'll be proud of you."

The "important ones" turned from Tom and stepped up to the window of the engine cab. Tom couldn't pile wood now. He had to listen to what they were saying. There was Mr. Gates with his hat in his hand.

"I take my hat off to you," he was saying to Engineer Bill. "You're doing what you said you'd do — bringing her home under her own steam!"

"You didn't doubt my word, by any chance, did you?" asked Engineer Bill, ready to flare up and get mad at a minute's notice. Then he must have seen the soot streaks. Anyway, he burst into a loud guffaw. "You're a sight, man! 'Puffing billy' certainly puffed some dirt on you!"

"He's no dirtier than the rest of us," laughed Mayor Hastings. "Man, man, what a ride you are giving us! The cinders rained down on that roof like hail!"

"You sent sparks enough in at the window to set fire to my newspaper," added Tom's father.

"The coach rocked, all right," laughed Mr. Gates, forgetting that he was the president of the railroad and entering into the fun. "But it was not the kind of rock that would put you to sleep. It's time we stopped making better engines and did something for the comfort of the passengers."

"Put screens in the windows," called one of the men.

"Take the red plush off the seats in the summer-time," called another, "and put some springs in the seats while you're about it."

"A few more tin cups chained to the drinking-water tank wouldn't be a bad idea," Tom's father broke in again. "A dozen thirsty people can't drink out of one cup at the same time."

"Whatever we do, we'll keep the padlock on the stove in the corner," chuckled Mr. Gates. "I wouldn't change that for anything."

"Well, gentlemen," said Engineer Bill with a twinkle in his eye, "it's your railroad, and I'm glad you're thinking up ways to improve it."

"Anyway, there's no reason for blaming a good engineer," laughed Mayor Hastings. "How long will we be held up on this siding, Bill?"

"Until Number 9 comes by and clears the track. Unfortunately," said Engineer Bill with a grin in Mr. Gates's direction, "trains going east have the right of way over trains going west. We can't go until the board's up and the track's clear, not even for the president of the railroad."

One by one the men wandered back to the coaches out of the blazing heat of the open prairie. Tom and Pierre climbed back into the engine cab.

"Coming with us, son?" asked Tom's father soberly, as he left the engine and started back to the coach. Tom didn't answer. He just looked.

Now, while Big Bill polished the brass fittings

of the engine cab, Pierre fed the yawning mouth of the firebox. Steam hissed steadily from the pop valve of the boiler.

"It's a good thing I'm not like the fireman on the *Best Friend of Charleston*," laughed Pierre.

"*Best Friend of Charleston!* What was that? An engine?" asked Tom.

"One of the first engines in America!" answered Pierre. "The fireman didn't like the noise of the hissing steam. So he fastened down the pop valve tight! Some people say he even sat on it."

"And the boiler blew into a thousand places," exclaimed Tom triumphantly. "It's not hard to tell how that story came out. Didn't he know that steam takes up sixteen hundred times as much room as the water that makes it?"

"I guess not," said Pierre. "Come to think of it, I've heard that story a hundred times, but I've never heard what happened to that feller."

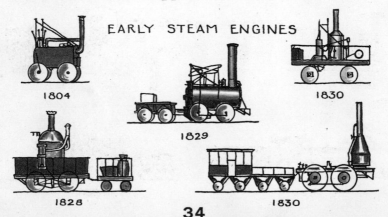

EARLY STEAM ENGINES

1804

1829

1830

1828

1830

"I'll tell you," announced Tom with conviction. But Pierre never found out how Tom settled the matter because just at that minute Number 9's whistle sounded from down the track — one long blast.

"She's coming, and she's going to stop!" shouted Tom. "Keep your eye on the board, Pierre, keep your eye on the board!"

Down the main track from the westward came a train pulled by a coal-burning engine with a tall, straight smokestack. Tom was hardly conscious of its coming. His eyes were fixed on the arm of the semaphore which extended out at right angles from the pole by the side of the track. Just as the train slipped by and came to a stop on the main track beyond the siding, ready to back into the siding when the *Pioneer* was again on its way, the arm of the semaphore shot into an upright position, parallel with the pole.

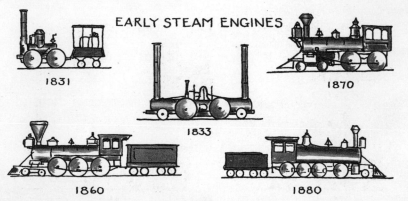

EARLY STEAM ENGINES

1831

1833

1870

1860

1880

"Board's up! The block's clear! Time to go!" shouted Tom. Back along the track he could see the conductor standing on the step of the coach, calling "All aboard" and giving the signal to start. Engineer Bill could see the conductor, also, as he leaned from the engine cab. The big brass bell of the *Pioneer* rang and rang as Fireman Pierre pulled on the bell cord. Two blasts of the whistle and the *Pioneer* was again on its way.

"Now for the homestretch," said Engineer Bill, as "puffing billy" left the siding for the main track.

Once again the faraway distances before them slipped away into the widening distances behind, and thoughts of his grandfather made Tom remember what Engineer Bill had said.

"A railroad doesn't make a town," he said with a thoughtful look in his blue eyes. "The railroad didn't make Hastings. My grandfather did."

"Come, now, lad," boomed Engineer Bill, a note of amused disagreement in his voice.

"Yes he did, too!" insisted Tom, hurrying on and allowing no time for argument. "He came west in a covered wagon when there wasn't even one cabin in the valley of the Big Turtle. He knew it was a good place for a town, and so he built a lumber mill. Then he cut down trees and sawed lumber so that other people could build homes, too. He's the one who made the town!"

"One thing is certain! He'll never need anyone to stick up for him while you're around," said Engineer Bill with a kindly chuckle. "Upon second thought, lad, perhaps you're right. I'm just an old railroad man who thinks an engine can do anything. Suppose we put it this way. Your grandfather made the town, and the railroad helped him make it the kind of town he wanted it to become. How will that suit you?"

"That's right," said Tom with conviction.

Now the *Pioneer* had slipped around a bend in the track and was headed southward through a lovely river valley. The river lay hot and still and apparently motionless between its gently sloping banks where woodland gave place to cornfields, and cornfields to ripening grain.

"Look, Pierre! It's the Big Turtle! We're almost home!" said Tom, tense with excitement.

Minutes went by. Then, suddenly and unexpectedly, up from the level stretches of prairie to the southward rose roofs, a few factory chimneys, and long lines of smoke — the unmistakable signs of a busy little town.

Before many minutes had passed, Tom was shouting, "Look, Engineer Bill, we're coming into the railroad yards. There's the roundhouse! There's the coach shop! There's the machine shop! I wonder if Old Joe will be the crossing watchman. He'd better not forget to lower the gates. All the people will be down at the depot. Wait and see!"

"If they aren't, they ought to be," boomed the big voice of Engineer Bill. "Here, lad, take the bell cord. Make them know that 'puffing billy' is coming home."

Never before had the brass bell of the *Pioneer* rung as it rang that July afternoon. Never had the whistle sounded so loudly. Down by the little red station, crowds of people lined the tracks and shouted a welcome. Engineer Bill leaned far out of the cab window, a smile of triumph on his face. And out from above and below Big Bill's sooty arms peered Tom, his hands pulling hard on the bell cord.

While Pierre threw another log into the firebox and soot and sparks and cinders rained down from the balloon-shaped smokestack upon the watching crowd, the *Pioneer* slid to a stop. The sign above the little red depot said "Hastings," and "puffing billy" was safely home.

Fourth of July

Fourth-of-July morning and the world was gay with dancing sunshine! A robin sang from the branch of a maple tree outside a bedroom window, and a woodpecker pecked with a will on the tin roof of the summer kitchen just below. From some not-too-faraway place drums beat and whistles blew. Yet Thomas Hastings, the Third, in the middle of the carved black-walnut bed, just turned over once and lay motionless.

Neither sunlight, an east window, nor the boom of Fourth of July could bring the stir and brightness of a summer's morning into that bedroom! Nothing could give a cheery look to the dull brown wallpaper, the heavy marble-topped dresser and table, and the long curtains which began at the window tops and reached out over the carpet-covered floor beneath.

"Tom! Tom! It's the Fourth of July! Aren't you ever going to get up? It's only three hours until the parade, and Mama says that you're to wash your ears."

A girl's voice, calling from the yellow pine doorway, did what the sunshine could not do. In the twinkling of an eye, Tom was staring down in

41

disgust at the match, the candle, and the heavy silver watch on the slippery horsehair seat of the chair by the bed. Hadn't he put those things there so that he could tell time in the middle of the night? Hadn't he put them there so that he would be up by four in the morning? And now look — seven o'clock! Three hours of Fourth-of-July fun gone already! What luck!

He dashed over, pulled aside the long lace curtains, pushed up the window, threw open the shutters, and leaned as far out as he could without tumbling on his head. Next door, at his Uncle Jim's house, someone was blasting away on a horn, running a drumstick back and forth along the white picket fence, and making a grand noise. Even his cousin Jim was up before him!

Tom's head was awhirl. His thoughts popped like firecrackers. One long black stocking on! Where was the other? Who stole his buttonhook? Who invented button shoes, anyway? Boots were the thing! Boots you could pull on! But not boots for a parade! Not when you're one of the principal actors!

Use his head! That's what a fellow must do! Don't let anybody make you dress all over again! Put on your "Sunday best" so that your mother will say, "Why, Tommy! How grand you look! Come here and let me fix your tie. I couldn't have done better if I had dressed you myself." Put on your "Sunday best" and hold your breath until your father gives in. "What kind of monkeyshines do you call this, Tom? You can't feed horses and clean out a barn in that outfit. We'll let it go for once, young man, but don't try that trick a second time — not around here!"

Astonishing how fast a boy can move when he wants to! By this time Tom was diving into the big dresser drawer. Blue — no! Brown — no! White to suit his mother! The one his Aunt Sally had made on her new sewing machine! Like a flash two long, freckled arms slipped into a stiff, starched blouse, and Tom was tying a wide red-silk tie in a big, soft bow under his chin.

Now for his hair! Oh, yes — ears! Huh, Mary just made that up! His mother hadn't said a word about ears. How could she? Hadn't she scrubbed the skin off him last night, getting off the soot

JEWEL STAND   BASKETS   EYEGLASSES   NEEDLE-CASE   TOWELS

TOWEL RACK   WASHBOWL AND PITCHERS   WORKBASKET

that he hadn't even budged? Ears can't get dirty in bed! Still — better not take any chances!

This time Tom's whirling thoughts carried him over to the washstand by the wall. Down slipped the water from the blue-flowered pitcher into the blue-flowered bowl, and off came the "setting hen" top to the soap dish. Then, standing as far back as he could, Tom churned the water into soapsuds with the handle of the hairbrush. Gingerly down into the soapsuds went the washcloth, and each ear got what Tom's mother called "a lick and a promise." Gingerly down into the blue jar on the floor went the soapsuds, and Tom wiped the brush

handle on the red-and-white towel on the towel rail at the side of the washstand. "Huh," thought Tom. "That's how a towel should look — all wet wrinkles but no dirt!"

Now for his hair! Wet it! Plaster it down! Down went the hairbrush into the blue-flowered pitcher! A gingerly shake — a brush — and Tom was ready for high adventure.

Two steps at a time and a slide down the black-walnut bannister! Tom landed on his feet on the thick-piled carpet among the patches of red, yellow, and blue light made by the squares of colored

WOMEN'S CLOTHES

glass round the big double doors at the end of the hallway.

The next minute he was walking soberly and quietly to his place at the breakfast table. There behind the big silver coffeepot sat his mother. Her hair was piled high on her head in many little curls, and still more hair hung at her neck in a very fashionable waterfall.

The tight basque of Mother's blue print dress had long, tight sleeves, and it buttoned down the front with little red glass buttons. There was a white lace collar at her throat and lace ruffles at the ends of her sleeves.

Even twelve-year-old Mary had something about her which suggested a holiday morning. Her hair was not braided, but hung long and loose and smoothly brushed about her shoulders, and the round comb which held it in place was her "Sunday best" with tiny bits of glass along the edge for decoration. As for Father, only the Fourth of July could put that curl in the ends of his sandy brown mustache.

As Tom slipped into his cane-seated chair, smiling-faced Norah entered from the kitchen with a big dish of hot pancakes. Her skirt crackled as she walked, with the crackle of the six starched petticoats which she wore underneath.

Tom hadn't time to take his napkin from his silver napkin ring before things began to happen. "Why, Tommy! How grand you look!" exclaimed his mother. "What kind of monkeyshines do you call this?" began his father. But Tom, with his red tie retied, just ate pancakes and sausages and potatoes and ham and bread and jelly. He just ate and trusted to luck while he watched the rainbow lights the sun made as it shone through the glass prisms which hung from the shade of the hanging lamp above the table.

When everything turned out as it should have turned out, then was the time for Tom to begin.

GIRLS' CLOTHES   BABY DRESS   TOYS

"You're going to pick up Old Joe in the surrey, aren't you, Papa?" he asked with conviction.

"I hadn't thought of it," replied his father. "By the way, Tom, don't let me hear a son of mine calling him Old Joe. He is Mr. Burns to a boy like you. Suppose you remember it hereafter."

"Yes, sir," said Tom, hanging his head in embarrassment. "But some days his wooden leg hurts. You shouldn't expect an old engineer who lost his leg working for the railroad to walk to the parade, should you?"

"He doesn't live a stone's throw from the depot," Mr. Hastings started to say. Then, with a sudden change of heart, he added, "I suppose the old fellow would like a ride."

"Of course he would," said Tom's mother, "and there is plenty of room in the surrey. But how shall we let him know?"

"Don't you think, sir," suggested Tom, "that someone should be over at Mr. Burns's house early to make sure that he is ready on time? You see how it is! He hates a stiff shirt, and Mrs. Burns can't do much on account of her rheumatism. He likes to have me do things like finding his collar buttons and putting on his stiff cuffs. I won't get there in time to help if I have to walk away over to the other end of town. But if I had a nickel, I could ride with Music on the mule car. Then you could pick me up, too, when you come by with the surrey."

EGGCUPS   CASTER SET   FRUIT DISH   NAPKIN RINGS   COFFEE URN   GOBLET

"Well, of all things!" exclaimed Mr. Hastings, looking disgusted at one minute and smiling in spite of himself the next. "So that's the reason for this Sunday-go-to-meeting attire so early in the morning! Now, Mrs. Hastings, what do you think of your son? Young man, I have a good mind to make you clean that barn."

But Tom didn't clean the barn, and he did get the nickel. Before many minutes he was taking down his hat from the carved black-walnut hat-stand which stood in the hallway between the double outside doors and the double inside doors with the colored glass borders. He could hardly keep still long enough to say "Yes, ma'am" to his mother when she made him promise to keep clean, but he had plenty of time to grin at Mary, who was complaining loudly.

"Oh, he never has to do anything! I have to wash dishes and clean the lamp chimneys in this whole house, and he can have a ride on the mule car! It just isn't fair!"

Tom cleared the front steps with a bound. He raced down the stone walk past the rose arbor and the summerhouse on one side, and the statue of the big brown deer in the center of the wide, grassy lawn on the other.

The dust in the dirt road outside the gate was a foot thick. It lay white and powdery on the grass along the roadside. A few neighborhood cows, seeking a juicier breakfast, stood on the wooden sidewalk with their heads over the white picket fence.

"Shoo! Get out of here! Eat your own grass!" shouted Tom. He stopped long enough to send the cows a-flying, then hurried out to the stone horse block and held on to the iron ring in the iron horse's head on top of the hitching post. From this vantage point he could tilt his heels on the edge of the horse block and lean far out over the road without danger of falling in the dust. But look as he would, there was no mule car coming down the tracks from the south.

"Hello, Ruffles! Where are you going?" called Charlie Lane with a mischievous grin, as he hurried across the street with a pitcher of milk from Uncle Jim's barn.

IRON DOG IRON CHAIR HITCHING POSTS FOUNTAIN IRON DEER

"Come here, and I'll show you!" Tom called back.

"I can't!" shouted Charlie. "I've got to get this milk home safely for breakfast." Charlie was Tom's best friend, but that didn't keep the two boys from having a friendly squabble every once in a while. Perhaps Tom didn't exactly like to be called "Ruffles," and perhaps Charlie knew all too well what Tom meant when he said, "I'll show you!" Anyway, Charlie hurried home with the milk.

Just at that minute Mr. Gray, who owned the flour mill where Hastings Belle flour was made, came down the road in a smart, red-wheeled buggy. He was an old man, but he still loved a good trotter. The iron-gray horse he was driving was the best trotting horse in his stable and could do a mile in a minute and a half, so its owner said. Someday soon this horse was going to win a race.

"Hello, Tom," called Mr. Gray, pulling up at the horse block. "Hop up here beside me, and I'll show you a horse that can trot."

"I can't," called Tom. "I have to go to Pigeon Hill on the mule car."

Mr. Gray grinned an understanding grin, then disappeared in a cloud of dust.

Whistling Mule Car

Now Maple Avenue seemed strangely deserted. Not a person anywhere! Maple Avenue was the most fashionable street in town. In the early days there had been a stand of sugar maples here, an outcropping of the Big Woods. As the town grew and the streets extended southward, a road was cut through the maples. Now big trees lined the street on either side, and on this July morning the shady stretches of dusty road were a-quiver with spots of dancing sunlight.

All up and down the street beyond the trees and the white picket fences were wide, shady lawns with arbors and summerhouses and statues and uncomfortable-looking iron chairs. At the rear of the grassy lawns stood the tall, stately-looking houses, some of wood, some, like Tom's house, of the Cherry Red brick for which Hastings was famous, and which came directly from Joseph White's brickyard.

54

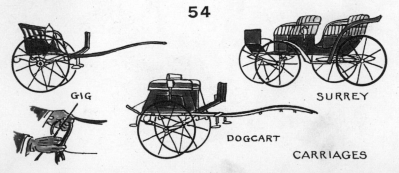

GIG

DOGCART

SURREY

CARRIAGES

Behind the houses were the barns and stables. In these stables, hidden from view on this July morning, were surreys and smart red-wheeled buggies and phaetons and even a victoria or two. In the stalls were the driving horses with their long legs and arching necks and spirited eyes. Most of the boys on Maple Avenue who were eleven years old, like Tom, had to spend long morning hours cleaning the barns, currycombing the horses until their coats shone like silk, and oiling and polishing the silver-mounted harnesses. So, of course, when you have to do all these things, you would much rather ride in a mule car.

It didn't take Tom long to explain the quietness of Maple Avenue to his own satisfaction. "They're finishing their work in the barns," he thought. "They're getting scrubbed up for the parade." He was feeling very pleased with himself that he was smarter than the rest of the boys, when Music and the mule car came into view.

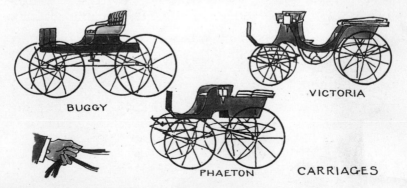

BUGGY

VICTORIA

PHAETON   CARRIAGES

Tom waved and halloed, then jumped right down into the dusty road and made for the track. There wasn't a passenger in the car, not one. Standing in the driver's place was a lively little old man with snapping black eyes, white chin whiskers, and thinning white hair. That man was Music, and he was Pierre's father — Pierre, the fireman on the *Prairie Flyer*.

"Hello, Tom, my boy!" he called, as Tom hopped in beside him. "What did I tell you, Thunder and Lightning? Didn't I tell you that two good brown mules couldn't help but pick up a passenger, and an important one, too? I hear you're to be a big man in the parade this morning, Tom. But where are you off to now?"

"I'm on my way to Pigeon Hill to help Old Joe — Mr. Burns, I mean — get ready," answered Tom. "I am going to ride with him in the cab of the *Pioneer*. But he's not going to be at the throttle! I am! He promised!"

Music whistled a gay giddap. Down the road toward town went the mule car with Music whis-

tling, Tom chattering, and Thunder and Lightning twitching their long ears backward as if they were taking in every word.

It was a good thing that Tom didn't have to remember to call Music Mr. DuSell. Tom didn't have to do that even when his father was around. Music was Music to everyone in Hastings, that is, except to Tom's grandfather, who still insisted on calling him Frenchy.

Frenchy had worked for Grandfather for years and years. He had cut down trees when the Big Woods were really big woods, and he had sawed logs in Grandfather's first sawmill. "The best workman I ever had or ever will have," Grandfather used to say. Now all that was left of the Big Woods was the large grove where the picnic grounds were, and most of the logs for Grandfather's lumberyard were shipped in by railroad. Now Frenchy was an old man, and Grandfather had found him an easier job driving the mule car.

The truth was that Frenchy had to drive the mule car. No one else could. Thunder and Lightning were very strong mules; but from the moment they were first hitched to the mule car, they made up their mule minds they weren't going to walk a track and pull a car. Most of the time they wouldn't even budge; but when they did, they kicked up their heels and ran. Driver after driver tried his best, only to give them up as a bad job.

"Their strength is better than their dispositions," chuckled Grandfather. "We'll have to get Frenchy to whistle in their ears."

Frenchy didn't really whistle in their ears, but he did whistle all the tunes he knew.

Then a most unusual thing happened. Before long those mules, who wouldn't budge an inch for anyone else, would fairly stand on their heads for Frenchy. They even had their own particular tunes. "Tramp, tramp, tramp, the boys are marching" would set them trotting right up the Main Street hill, and "Listen to the Mocking Bird" would ease them down again. "Old Dog Tray" would make them stand without twitching an ear when the crossing gates came down and the trains went by, and the first note of "When Johnny Comes Marching Home" would start them on the run for their own barn at night.

Almost overnight the mules became the town attraction. Someone began calling Frenchy "Music," and the name spread like wildfire. People came from far and near to ride the "whistling mule car." Frenchy really did a very fine business, except on this Fourth-of-July morning when everyone was getting ready for the parade.

Now Music and Tom and the mule car turned westward into Main Street, which had once been the old stagecoach road. There at the top of the Main Street hill, where the road sloped down into the valley of the Big Turtle River and the business streets of the town began, stood "The House on the Hill." That's what everyone called Tom's grandfather's house. That is what everyone had always called it since that long-ago day when some of the men still living in Hastings had helped with the house-raising.

"The House on the Hill" had changed with the years. A wing had been added to the east and another to the west, and in the rear was a new summer kitchen. The main part of the house was as Grandfather had first built it. The two big maples still shaded the wide stretches of grassy lawn, and the low brick wall still circled the well. There were homes in Hastings grander than this, with brick walls and wide verandas. But no other house faced the road so squarely. No other house gave such a straightforward welcome in the friendliness of its white paint and green shutters and its wide, small-paned windows.

This morning, as the mule car passed the white picket gate, Tom suddenly remembered the numberless times he had stood there with his father, looking up at the rambling old house. Something stirred deep down inside of Tom, a feeling quick and intense, the same feeling he always had when his father began:

"See those timbers, Tom! I remember seeing those timbers when they were still trees in the Big Woods. And those shingles! The few above the front door, different from the rest! Your grandfather has kept them there through all these years. I shaved those shingles in my father's first mill when I was as old as you are now."

But thoughts of the past soon gave way to thoughts of the present. "There's a great man staying in that house today," Tom exclaimed, as the car turned north into Lincoln Avenue, the street which bordered Grandfather's yard on the west. "He's the president of the railroad."

"Pooh!" grunted Music. "The Mayor of Hastings lives there, and that's more important."

Now the streetcar tracks led through a different part of town where the houses and yards were smaller. Cheerful-looking cottages lined the streets, with big vegetable gardens at their back doors and old-fashioned pink and yellow rosebushes bordering the grassplots in front. The white picket fences gave way to high board fences, not so beautiful to look upon except where the hollyhocks grew, but much better for keeping out cows and for carving initials.

There were few cows in the streets this morning. But boys were there, and girls, and beating drums, and tooting whistles, and many other small things which made a big noise. It took all Frenchy's musical power to get the mules either to come or to go through that part of town.

Finally the hoofs of the two brown mules were tramping out a hollow sound on the log flooring of the wooden bridge over Indian Creek. Now Tom and Music had come to the "Cross." The south side of Indian Creek belonged to everyone else in Hastings; but the north side was Pigeon Hill, and you didn't live there unless you worked for the railroad.

Pigeon Hill was the worry of Tom's mother's life. "Why do you want to be forever over there?" she asked continually. "Can't you find a single boy on this side of the creek to play with?"

But Tom knew why he wanted to be on Pigeon Hill. There were machinists and boilermakers and coach carpenters living on Pigeon Hill, and they knew all there was to know about engines. They were railroad men with no liking for horses. So they lived close together within easy walking dis-

tance of the shop yards. There were engineers
and firemen and brakemen among them, and the
callboys could raise an engine crew in half an hour
even on a cold winter night.

The minute the mule car left the bridge, things
became more lively. Now there were men as well
as boys and girls outside the well-kept cottages.

Some were pitching horseshoes, others were watching a friendly wrestling match. Some were already on their way to town to find good places from which to view the parade, and still others were just loafing, enjoying a day's rest from their hard work in "The Shops." But there was not one among them who did not take time to call, "Hello, Tom! How's the engineer this morning? Good luck, boy! Pigeon Hill will be cheering for you!"

Halfway down the High Street hill, Tom jumped from the car and started on the run for a little yellow cottage with green shutters, standing in the shade of an old walnut tree. A bustling little old lady was shaking a duster in the doorway.

"Is Mr. Burns ready?" called Tom, as he raced along. "My father is coming for him in the surrey."

"Ready, child!" exclaimed Mrs. Burns, shaking her hands, her head, and the duster all at the same time. "He's been ready since six this morning, and in my way and under my feet ever since. I've just shooed him out to smoke his pipe in the back yard before he drives me crazy."

Tom raced around the house and stopped dead in his tracks. There on the seat which circled the walnut tree sat Mr. Burns, smoking his corncob pipe. There he sat in *blue overalls* and a *blue shirt* with an *old engineer's cap* on his head.

"Why!" exclaimed Tom, when he could finally talk. "I thought you were ready! The surrey will be here at any minute."

When Old Joe saw Tom's look of consternation, his own face was one big question mark. "What's the matter with me, lad?" he asked, looking himself all over. "I *am* ready!"

"Oh!" said Tom, not realizing what he was saying. "Are you going, looking like that?"

For a second it looked as though Old Joe would flare up in a terrible temper. But the next moment he was shaking with laughter, and his wrinkles sank deeper and deeper.

"So you thought you'd find me in a boiled shirt," he chuckled through his tears. "Lad, lad! What would 'puffing billy' think of me if I climbed into her cab decked out like that? I'd be the laughing-stock of the town."

It took Tom a minute or two; then like a flash he understood. "Of course you would!" he grinned. "I wouldn't be dressed up, either, if I could help it. But I wouldn't be here if I weren't, that's one thing certain."

"And now," said Mr. Burns, "I've a matter to settle with you. Two hours of good work I had to put in last night, and all on your account. Didn't you and Engineer Bill say that you had polished the brass on the *Pioneer?* You don't know what a shine is! Now, when I was an engineer and not just a crossing watchman sitting in a shanty beside the tracks and letting down gates, I — "

Old Joe might just as well have saved his breath. Tom wasn't even listening. He had already started on a continual run from the tree to the gate and back again, looking for the surrey. By the time he caught the first glimpse of it, he actually had a path worn in the grassy lawn.

But there it was at last, splendid in its shiny black paint and red wheels. The gold fringe round the heavy cloth top was swinging in the breeze, and the two iron-gray horses were stepping high.

On the back seat sat Mother and Mary. Mother's dress was all little silk ruffles, and over her head she held a tiny lace parasol. On top of her curls was a tiny hat with a yellow plume, tilting back over her waterfall in the very latest fashion. Mary looked lovely, too, in her dress made almost like

SMOKER'S FRIENDS

Mother's, her pink sash, and her little lace mitts. There were plumes, also, in the pink ribbon-band of her tiny straw hat. Father on the front seat looked splendid but very hot, in his high hat, his coat with the black satin on the collar, and his tight yellow gloves.

"Mr. Burns," said Father, with a very straight face, as he stepped down to help Old Joe into the surrey, "I congratulate you. Never in my life have I seen a better-dressed engineer. I was very glad to be able to do the extra work in the barn

this morning so that Tom could help you into that stiff shirt."

Of course everyone laughed, even Tom, though his face was as red as a cherry. But a few minutes later he was seated on the front seat of the surrey between Father and Mr. Burns, and his embarrassment was all forgotten. Father's perfectly matched team of high-stepping horses was kicking up the dust of High Street hill on the way to the depot. The parade was still before him, and Tom's heart beat high with expectation.

69

FLY NET

HAT

BLANKET

CURRYCOMBS

NOSE GUARD

Parade

Dust, July heat, and the thrill of expectation! Buildings gaily decorated with streamers of red, white, and blue! Flags waving, horns blowing, drums beating! Hastings was ready for the big parade.

Each road leading into town was bringing its share of hurrying people. Farm buggies lined the quieter side streets. Horses, half-asleep in the sunshine, were stamping off flies at the hitching rails. A few of the fortunate ones had hats on their heads with holes for their ears, and gaily fringed fly nets to keep them from stamping. But the greater number, with unprotected heads, just stamped and grew sleepier in the heat and the sunshine.

Down on Broadway and River Street, the business streets which ran north and south along the banks of the Big Turtle River, excitement was running high. People lined the wooden sidewalks in front of the few important-looking brick buildings and the many one-story, wooden shops which tried to look important with their high false fronts. People in their "Sunday best," pushing, crowding, calling gay helloes as they picked their way across the cobblestone crossings at the street corners! People moving and waiting, moving and waiting!

Over at the little red depot everything was bustling confusion. In the street beside the station the parade was already in line, awaiting the signal to swing into motion. Hurrah! The signal at last, and carried along by the lilt of marching music, the parade swung south into Broadway.

First came the band, splendid in brass-buttoned uniforms of red and blue, with fifes tooting, bugles blowing, and the fat little drummer boy beating out a rat-a-tat-tat with his drumsticks.

Behind the band, reaching from one side of the wide, dusty street to the other, walked a line of

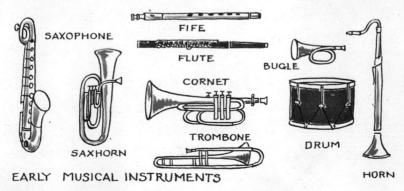

SAXOPHONE

FIFE

FLUTE

BUGLE

CORNET

SAXHORN

TROMBONE

DRUM

EARLY MUSICAL INSTRUMENTS

HORN

HASTINGS
RAIL
25 YEARS

railroad men carrying high the banner which announced in letters for all to see,

HASTINGS, LAKE SHORE, AND WESTERN RAILROAD
25 YEARS OF GROWING

Following the banner came a long wooden platform mounted on wagon wheels and drawn by four powerful farm horses. On the platform, bedecked with streamers of red, white, and blue, her brass fittings shining as brass never shone before, rode "puffing billy." No soot nor sparks nor cinders rained from her balloon-shaped smokestack this morning. The glass in her headlight, the carved wood of her engine cab, and the gold lettering of her name, *The Pioneer*, were polished until they gleamed in the sunlight. Far out from the window of the cab, waving his engineer's cap with a will, leaned Old Joe, "puffing billy's" first engineer. And at the throttle, beaming with dignity and importance, stood Tom.

The cheers of the watching crowd were deafening, but high and clear above the rest of the cheers came the shouts of Pigeon Hill.

"Hello, Joe! How does it seem to be in an engine cab again? Remember the days when you wouldn't take that engine out in the rain? They don't make engineers like you these days. Watch out, Tom! Don't open that throttle! 'Puffing billy' might run off the track!"

Just as the band was passing Dan Cutter's cigar store where the wooden Indian in the feathered

STORE SIGNS

LIVERY STABLE

CIGAR STORE

FURRIER SHOP

74

headdress was holding out a handful of wooden cigars, the fifes and the bugles struck up another air. With one accord, the milling crowds took up the tune.

"I've been working on the railroad,
All the livelong day.
I've been working on the railroad,
To pass the time away."

Even the Mayor of Hastings and the president of the railroad, riding behind the *Pioneer* in the victoria drawn by Grandfather's two sleek, brown carriage horses, joined in the singing. On and on went the song, and over and over.

"Don't you hear the bugles blowing,
Rise up so early in the morn,
Don't you hear the captain shouting,
Dinah, blow your horn."

The song resounded from every surrey and side-car and phaeton and buggy which followed the victoria in the line of march. Each gaily decorated carriage was filled to overflowing with those people in Hastings who, in the days gone by, had had something to do with bringing the railroad to Hastings Mills.

It was only when the last carriage came into view that the singing changed to amused laughter. There, near the end of the parade, dusty and queer-looking and much the worse for wear as a result of years of standing in John Hunt's livery stable, came an old brown stagecoach. No effort had been made to decorate it with streamers, to clean its paint, or to polish its door handles. Today it was pulled by the oldest and saddest-looking horses in all the country round. "COME FOR A RIDE. I CAN GO LIKE LIGHTNING," read the big signs which covered its doors.

Lumbering along behind the stagecoach came a covered wagon drawn by two slow-moving oxen. "TEN MILES A DAY BUT WE BROUGHT YOU HERE," said the sign on the ox yoke. Behind the covered wagon walked another line of railroad men with a banner which announced,

HASTINGS BEGAN WITH A
COVERED WAGON BUT
THE IRON HORSE MADE HER GROW

Down Broadway went the parade past the barbershop with its red-and-white barber pole and the bootblack stand near the doorway. On past Silas Hood's store where the wooden mortar and pestle

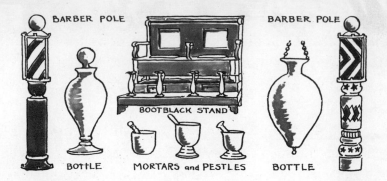

BARBER POLE BARBER POLE

BOOTBLACK STAND

BOTTLE MORTARS and PESTLES BOTTLE

on the sidewalk, and the green glass bottle in the
window with the light shining behind it, announced
to everyone who passed that this was a drugstore!

Just as "puffing billy" was passing the jewelry
store with the gold-painted wooden watch above
the doorway, Tom caught sight of his cousin Jim,
cheering loudly. Mother, Mary, and Aunt Sally
waved from the second-story window of the brick
building where Uncle Jim had his furniture store.
Still farther along under the great, high-buttoned
shoe which hung above the door of the cobbler
shop, Old Joe caught a glimpse of Mrs. Burns.
She was bumping into everyone unthinkingly while
she shaded her head from the sun with a big black
umbrella.

On went the parade past the splendid wooden
horse on the sidewalk in front of the harness shop.
On ordinary days any attempt to touch the silver-
mounted harness or the gold-fringed fly net would

have brought John Sawyer to the door on the run. But today the horse's back and even the top of his gray head were crowded with long-legged boys.

Now the parade turned west into Fox Street past the lumberyard on the left, and on the right "The Field House," the big wooden hotel with wide verandas extending about it on all sides, both upstairs and down. Today every vantage point on the verandas was filled with people.

Another minute and the band was rumbling into the hollow darkness of the covered wooden bridge over the east branch of the Big Turtle River.

FIVE DOLLARS FINE
FOR RIDING OR DRIVING
FASTER THAN A WALK ON THIS BRIDGE

So read the sign over the entrance.

Just as the *Pioneer* passed the little windows in the center of the bridge, Tom heard the long toot-toot of an engine whistle and caught a fleeting glimpse of a train moving across the wooden trestles of the railroad bridge to the south.

TEASHOP

SIGNS
AND
SYMBOLS

JEWELER
R.C.SMITH

TOBACCO SHOP

SHOESHOP

"It's Big Bill and Pierre," he cried excitedly, "and they're waving like everything! I can't see them, but I know that they are!"

"Just think of it," he burst forth after a minute. "The *Prairie Flyer* went right through Hastings, and there was so much cheering that we didn't even hear her. I suppose there wasn't a person at the depot except the station agent to watch her go through. That's the first time that ever happened. I'll bet Big Bill and Pierre wish that they could see this parade. I'll bet they wish they were in this engine cab."

"I reckon they do," said Old Joe. "But when you're a railroad man, you don't do what you want to do. You keep your mind on your job, and you keep the trains running. Don't forget that!"

All the people in Hastings weren't on Broadway, by any means. Island Avenue, which connected the bridge over the east branch of the river with the one over the west, was black with people. Boys were perched on every inch of the hitching rail which stretched the full length of the street in front of the woolen mill. One man, tired of holding his baby, had found her a seat on the head of the big stuffed bear which guarded the entrance to the Hat and Furrier Shop.

In the door of Mr. Steel's grocery store stood the
little fat butcher in his long white apron. His
bald head was aglow, and his face was as red as a
cherry from cheering. He had been going from
door to door since early morning, selling meat
from his big yellow meat wagon. Now he stood
between the two big barrels which Mr. Steel

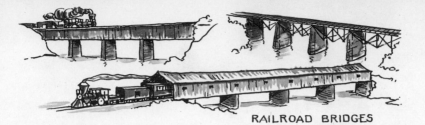

RAILROAD BRIDGES

always kept on the sidewalk. You could help yourself if you wanted to, but watch out! Those barrels were filled with very sour pickles.

No sooner had the band left the second covered bridge than the fifes and bugles burst into the spirited music of "Yankee-Doodle," and the parade turned north into River Street.

Now, for a moment, Tom almost forgot his dignity and importance. He was too busy staring down over the heads of the people into the window of a little brown shop which was below street level, so that you had to walk down steps to get into it. Fastened over the door was piece after piece of tissue paper cut into long strips. When the door opened, the tissue paper waved in every direction and shooed out the flies. On most days the tissue paper was pink and green, but today it was red, white, and blue.

In the window of the little brown candy shop, because that is what it was, were molasses candy, and long ropes of licorice, and red-and-white peppermint sticks, and wintergreen hearts, and little

82

tins of pink candy which you called ice cream. Tom couldn't really see all these things, but he knew they were there. One glimpse at that store and Tom was certain that it was time for this parade to be over.

On rolled "puffing billy" past the Hastings Belle flour mill on the right and the best livery stable in town on the left. Of course it was the best livery stable! Wouldn't John Hunt rent a horse and buggy for a whole afternoon for only a dollar? And didn't he claim that there wasn't a horse in his stable that needed a driver? "Give any horse of mine his head, and he'll fetch you home again." That's what John Hunt used to say, but he always grinned when he said it.

At the corner of New York Street was the hardware store with chairs to tilt back against the building and a pump or two cluttering up the sidewalk in front. There, too, was Mrs. Hall's bakeshop, and in the window was an enormous wedding cake all decorated with pink roses.

COVERED BRIDGE

Now the parade turned east to enter the long covered bridge which extended away across the river north of the island. Sparrows flew from their nests among the eaves with a wild flutter of wings as "puffing billy" rumbled over the planks of the long bridge. On marched the parade from darkness into sunlight, then drew to a stop with a flourish of drumsticks in front of the little red depot.

For the next few minutes all there was to be seen was streams of people hurrying up New York Street hill. People gathered like flies about the hitching rails in the side streets. Buggies began to dash up and down in clouds of dust. Gray horses kept pace with black horses, and brown horses with dappled-gray. Miles of horses and buggies on their way up the hill, then north beyond Pigeon Hill to Hastings Grove where the rest of the Fourth-of-July celebration was to be held!

The instant the band stopped playing, Tom had a sinking feeling. Like a flash he realized that he should be anywhere except in that engine cab.

"Puffing billy" was the center of attraction. Of course she had to go to the picnic grounds where everyone could climb into her cab, ring her bell, and look her over. But every horse in town would be at the Grove before these four lumbering farm horses could pull this heavy platform even to the top of the hill. This was a pretty fix to be caught in! He wished to goodness he were riding behind his father's high-stepping grays.

"Don't you think I should go ahead and choose a good place for 'puffing billy,' Mr. Burns?" he asked with eager conviction. "With all these buggies going to the same place, there won't be an inch of room left. We don't want the *Pioneer* to be pushed off in any old corner."

"What kind of engineer are you," boomed Old Joe, "deserting your engine before the end of the run? That's not the stuff an engineer is made of."

Tom flushed to the roots of his sandy hair. Not another word did he say about leaving the engine cab. But try as he would, he couldn't resist a continual call to Mr. Bell, who was driving the horses. "Can't these old horses go a bit faster? Not one bit?"

Unfortunately, Tom was right in his thinking. There wasn't an inch of space left under the long horse sheds by the time "puffing billy" reached the Grove. Horses munching away from their feed bags were tied to every available tree at the edge of the Grove. Even the sad-looking stage horses were enjoying their oats.

Yet Tom need not have worried. In front of the long tent where the church ladies were serving a hot chicken dinner — all you could eat for only a quarter — was a place of state reserved for the *Pioneer*. Though the waiting line of hungry people reached almost to the northern end of the Grove, there were two seats for Tom and Mr. Burns at the head table across from Grandfather and Grandmother and the president of the railroad. Why shouldn't there be two reserved seats? After all, weren't Tom and Mr. Burns two important actors in the parade?

In between juicy mouthfuls of chicken, Grandfather and Grandmother and Old Joe talked of the good old days. Tom amused Mr. Gates with the statement that when he was a man, he wouldn't stop until he had made an engine that could go seventy-five miles an hour.

"If you do, you'll have to make better track than we have today for it to run on," said Mr. Gates, laughing heartily.

When dinner was over, there were three-legged races, and wrestling matches, and horseshoe throwing, and a dozen other exciting things to take up the time. But when the buglers and the fife players and the fat little drummer took their places in the bandstand, then it was time for the speeches to begin.

The president of the railroad had the first speech. He looked very grand in his cutaway coat, his fancy brocaded vest, his high collar, and black silk stock. When he was not using his right hand to help his speech along, he was putting his gold-rimmed nose glasses on and off.

He began by talking about Fourth of July and the Declaration of Independence, but before long he was talking about Grandfather. Now Tom and Jim, sitting on the plank seat in front of the bandstand, stopped wiggling and really began to listen. Now there was something to listen to. It was their own grandfather Mr. Gates was talking about.

Twenty-five years ago today, when Grandfather drove the first spike in the first tie on the Hastings, Lake Shore, and Western Railroad, the town of Hastings declared its independence, too. Independence from bad roads and bad weather, from slow-moving farm wagons as the only way to get its goods to market! Now Cherry Red bricks and Hastings Belle flour were known in the four corners of the land. Why? Because the railroad was there to carry them!

All day long the crowds had been cheering at the sight of the *Pioneer*, and rightly so. But now the time had come to cheer for the one who had made the *Pioneer* possible. The man who twenty-five years ago wouldn't let other men in Hastings sleep nights until they agreed to help him with his wild plans! The man who made them put their hands down into their pockets and keep them there until they brought them out with money enough to make the railroad possible! Everyone knew whom Mr. Gates was talking about. The real pioneer — Thomas Hastings!

It may be that Mr. Gates was not through talking, but whatever else he wanted to say was lost in great waves of shouting and cheering which died away only to begin all over again. Then, somehow, Grandfather was in the speaker's place in the bandstand, Grandfather with his soft white hair and beard, his clear blue eyes, and his strong, quiet, kindly face. Suddenly everyone was still, and Grandfather was smiling a slow smile through his wrinkles.

If he had kept the men of Hastings awake nights and taken money from their pockets, he was hearing about it for the first time. Strange "goings on" for a sensible man! Strange, too, that he had no feeling of regret! If the future held anything as important as the coming of the railroad, he would do the same thing all over again. So would they all.

There were a few people left who had stood with him here more than thirty years ago, in the midst of unbroken prairie and the dark stretches of the Big Woods. If their dreams had come true, if the town they had hoped for had arisen in the valley of the Big Turtle, it was not his "doings" alone, but the "doings" of all who had worked with him. It was hard to imagine that anything better than a railroad could ever happen to any town. If the future did hold better things, he hoped there would always be someone by the name of Hastings to help the good work along.

"He means us! He means us when we're men!" whispered Jim, tense with excitement, nudging Tom in the ribs and looking at him with great, shining eyes.

Again the waves of cheering rose and fell. Crowds surged about the bandstand to talk to Grandfather and Mr. Gates. Minutes passed. The band began to play, and people on the outskirts of the crowd turned their steps toward home. The Fourth-of-July celebration was over.

"Good-by, Tom! Stop on Pigeon Hill on your way home!" called one boy's voice and then another's.

But for once Pigeon Hill had lost its attraction. There are times when boys like to be with men, listening to men's talk and planning the great things they themselves will do when they are grown up. Today was one of those times. Before long Tom and Jim were sitting with their cousin Sam on the slippery horsehair sofa in Grandmother's

parlor, trying to keep themselves from sliding off
by digging their toes into the thick, piled carpet
with the big red roses. All the time they were
digging, the carved grapevine on the top of the
sofa was making big dents in their necks and
shoulders.

Tom's father, entering the room, found them
there and started to send them scurrying. "What
are you doing here? Run along and be quick about
it," he said in a decided way. But Grandmother,
who understood boys, soon put a stop to that.
"Be still now!" she said to Tom's father, as if he
were four years old and not forty. "There are

times when it is good for boys to be listening, and
this is one of them." In the end, the boys found
better seats on the stairs in the hall. There they
sat, peering eagerly through the stair rails.

Grandmother's parlor was a grand place, almost
too grand to sit in. She seldom opened it except
when company came. The wallpaper. was white
with big gold roses. On the walls were big black-
and-white pictures of Grandmother and Grandfather in heavy gold frames. At the windows were
long lace curtains which swept the floor, and velvet
curtains held back with heavy gold cords.

The rosewood chairs were covered with horse-

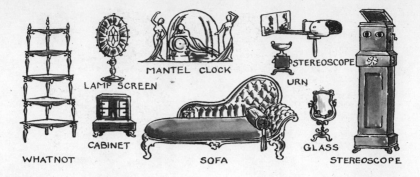

WHATNOT · LAMP SCREEN · MANTEL CLOCK · STEREOSCOPE · URN · CABINET · SOFA · GLASS · STEREOSCOPE

hair, and the marble-topped center table was almost hidden from sight under a heavy gold-colored tablecloth. On the table was the family album with its red velvet covers, and Grandmother's autograph album with gaily decorated pages upon which you wrote verses.

There were stuffed birds and a brown marble clock on the shelf above the white marble fireplace. In one corner of the room was a whatnot, filled with little figures of boys and girls and numberless other things which Grandmother called bric-a-brac. Yes, it was a grand place, Grandmother's parlor.

Before long the room was filled with men and talk and laughter. Now the boys listened breathlessly to thrilling tales of train wrecks and the bravery of engine crews. Story followed story, and the minutes went racing by. No one realized how late it was getting until Mr. White, the big black-

FURNITURE

DRESSING CASE

SOFA

WASTE-BASKET

FOOTSTOOL

TABLE   DESK   CHAIR

smith, raised his long legs from Grandfather's rocker and said, as he heaved a sigh, "A railroad can do most anything, but I've never heard tell of an engine that can milk cows or feed horses. Good day, gentlemen!"

The spell was broken. Another minute and every man in the room heard the call of the workaday world and was on his way home. Before long, barefooted Tom, in overalls, was pitching down hay from the haymow in his father's big barn.

But no workaday world could keep Tom from dreaming. His hands were busy with the hayfork, but his head was buzzing with ideas. Someday he'd be a great man, as great as his grandfather, or maybe greater. He'd make an engine that could go seventy-five miles an hour and a track to stand the speed. And who would be the first man to ride in the cab? Mr. Gates, because Mr. Gates thought it couldn't be done.

Bargains

It was a day or two after the Fourth of July. The early morning sun blazed from a cloudless sky, and the air above the gardens seemed to quiver with heat waves.

At the Banker Hastings home, breakfast and the work in the barns were over. Father, on his way to the bank, had already stepped into his smart, red-wheeled buggy drawn by Star, his sleek, brown trotter. Tom, in a circle of pails, an upturned bucket of water in his hand, was priming the wooden pump by the kitchen door.

The empty bucket dropped with a bang, and Tom set to work on the pump handle in an apparent effort to pump the well dry. Up, down! Faster, faster! A hollow gurgle, a sucking sound, then a gush of water from the wooden nozzle!

One pail for drinking! One pail for cooking! Water to fill every pitcher in every washbowl in the whole house! Well water is hard water and not meant for washbowls, but what can you do when the cistern runs dry? You can't pull soft water out of a dry cistern. One pail for scrubbing! And today — water to wash dozens of fruit jars and jelly glasses, and an extra tub or two just in case!

If Tom was trying to pump the well dry in the space of a minute, he had his own good reasons. At that moment there wasn't a thought in his mother's head except the thoughts which go with making beds and setting a house to rights. But he must be off and away before she had time to get ideas. Otherwise he might spend the morning in a sizzling hot kitchen beside a red-hot cookstove. Otherwise he might find himself with an apron round his neck, pitting the selfsame cherries which had already cost him a day's fun to pick.

Of course, if that happened, he could shoot cherry juice at the walls or maybe into Mary's eye. Then Norah might tell him to stop his grumbling and run along. He was of no use, anyway. After all, a man has to think up ways to protect himself, and pitting cherries is no man's job. On the other hand, his mother might threaten to bring him to his senses with a good hard slap. One never knows how things are going to turn out. It's safer not to let things get started.

"Tom! Tom!" called his cousin Jim, breaking into Tom's thinking as he dashed around the corner of the house. "Charlie Lane has his uncle's bicycle, and he's showing off in front of all the boys on Maple Avenue! Come on! Come on and see!"

"Here! Take this pump handle! I've got to fill the wood box!" cried Tom, fairly pushing Jim up to the pump and putting the handle into his hands. "Do you think he'll give us a ride?"

"A ride! I should say not! His uncle warned him not to let another boy touch that bicycle, let alone ride it!" exclaimed Jim, beginning to pump with might and main without a thought as to what he was doing. Suddenly he stopped. "Say, why don't you get up early enough to do your own work? Every time I come over here, you've got something for me to do. Suppose you pump your own water. I'm going!"

"Aw! Can't you wait a minute? I'm through now!" begged Tom, dashing through the kitchen door with an armload of wood and hurrying to fill the last pail with a flourish. "I wish my father weren't so old-fashioned. Think of having an uncle with a bicycle! I asked Papa why he didn't buy a bicycle, and he said he preferred a good safe trotting horse. Imagine that!"

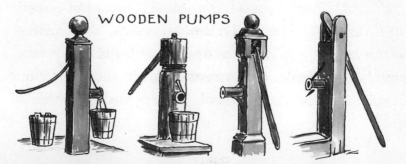

WOODEN PUMPS

By this time Jim was vaulting the gate in the white picket fence, and Tom was close at his heels. It was a long distance from the house to the front gate. So you can't blame Tom if he didn't hear a voice calling from an upstairs window, "Tom-m-m! I want you!"

Charlie Lane's uncle was a dandy. That's what the older people in Hastings said about him. They even said that he would come to no good end. Mayor Hastings was the only one who took John's part. "We need someone around here to put ginger into the rest of us," the mayor used to say. "Give John time, and he'll change his ways." In the meantime, John Lane dressed in the latest fashion — in tight-fitting trousers, fancy vests, big bow ties, and collars so high that they came right up under his ears.

When John Lane saw a picture in the paper of one of those newfangled things called a bicycle, with an enormous wheel in front and a very small wheel behind, well — John Lane had to have one.

He had a great time learning to ride. In the first place, he had to climb onto a picket fence, or up some steps, or part way up a hill, to be able to swing his leg over the big wheel and get onto the seat. Keeping his balance was no easy matter,

EARLY BICYCLES

1866

1880

1875

and a fall from that high in the air was no easy
fall. Moreover, there wasn't a long stretch of
level sidewalk in the whole of Hastings for him
to ride on. In almost every block there was a
place where the sidewalk rose to a higher level or
sank to a lower one in a series of steps, and bicycles
were never intended to climb steps. As for the
roads, the dust might hide the hills and hollows,
but it did nothing whatsoever to make rough going
smoother.

John Lane was sure that the moment his bicycle
appeared in town, all his friends would have bicycles,
too. Together they might form a bicycle club.
But that isn't what happened. Maybe his friends
didn't have the money, or maybe they wanted to
save what they did have. Anyway, there continued
to be only one bicycle in Hastings. Before long,
John Lane lost interest in riding all by himself.
Perhaps that is why he was willing to let his nephew,
Charlie, try his hand at the bicycle.

Charlie was twelve and very long-legged. "Longshanks" — that's what the boys called him. Now, for once, his long legs were coming in handy.

The minute Tom and Jim reached the road, they saw Charlie far up the street, perched on the crossrail of a picket fence, all ready to swing his leg over the big wheel and take off. Jim was up the street like lightning, his arms swinging in wide sweeps to help him along. Wise Tom dropped to a slower pace, his hands in his pockets, counting up his stock in trade.

Jackknife — no! Charlie had two knives. Top — no good! A bicycle rider wouldn't be caught dead spinning a top. Arrowheads — anyone could dig up a dozen of those old things down by the creek. Horse chestnut — huh! A fellow doesn't give away his luck, no matter what happens. Silver whistle — that might do it! Might get a fellow in trouble, too, when his father found out! Can't let that stop you at a time like this! Now he had it! There's an idea! Oh, he could never do that! Still — if he had to — if the whistle didn't work!

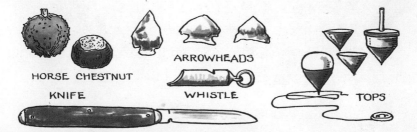

HORSE CHESTNUT

ARROWHEADS

KNIFE

WHISTLE

TOPS

By this time Prince Charlie was sailing triumphantly along, with every boy and girl on Maple Avenue running by his side. Dogs aplenty yelped and jumped in front of the big wheel. Charlie shouted to everyone to get out of the way. It was more exciting than a circus parade.

Just at the moment when Charlie began to wobble and seemed headed for a bad upset, he caught sight of Tom, swinging a whistle by a string.

"Too bad you haven't a whistle," said Tom in an unconcerned manner, as he reached up to help steady the wheel. "A whistle would clear the track all right."

"Let me take yours then!" exclaimed Charlie.

"Huh — not this whistle! It's silver! Don't you know that?" said Tom, leaning over to polish the whistle on the leg of his worn blue trousers.

"Why are you swinging it by a string then?" demanded Charlie. "You think I'm dumb! You think I'll trade a ride on this bicycle for that old whistle. Well, I won't! My Uncle John would fix me if he caught another boy on his bicycle."

"Didn't your Uncle John go to work this morning? How can he tell who's riding his bicycle?" inquired Tom hopefully.

"He may not see, but he'll hear about it all right," retorted Charlie. "Say, you think you're smart! You think you could ride this bicycle without even trying. It takes brains to do this! Anyway, I don't want your old whistle."

Now, Tom might have given up in despair. Things certainly looked hopeless. But he didn't give up. He went right on holding the bicycle for Charlie and helping him lift it up and down steps. All the time the bicycle was headed down Maple Avenue toward the edge of town.

At first other boys and girls joined the procession. But as time went on, Charlie's followers began to drop off, one by one. They knew in their hearts that there was no chance of a ride. They grew tired of watching someone else have all the fun. They wanted to have some fun of their own. Before long, Tom and Jim were the only ones left. Then, as they passed Mr. Gray's barn, Jim disappeared, also.

All at once Charlie got the idea that it was time to turn around and go home. Tom couldn't see the sense in that. Why not keep going in the same direction as long as the sidewalks lasted? Soon the two boys came to the outskirts of Hastings. Now Tom really began to get down to business.

"Not many people around here," he remarked with an indifferent air, as he helped turn the bicycle round at the end of the last stretch of sidewalk. "A person could do most anything out here without being seen."

"Like riding this bicycle, I suppose," said Charlie wisely, "without my Uncle John hearing about it."

"Maybe," admitted Tom. "I might be thinking that, and I might be right about it, too." Still no offer of a ride from Charlie!

Suddenly Tom seemed in a desperate hurry. He gave a quick start and snapped his fingers as if he had just remembered something.

"I hope you can manage that bicycle by yourself," he said. "I hope you can stop when you come to steps. I wouldn't want you to break an arm or leg — not away out here all by yourself. I've got to be going. I promised some boys that I'd go exploring down by the creek."

All the time Tom was talking, he stood tilted forward, his right hand in his pocket. Just as he was all set to go, out of that pocket came a —

There wasn't another compass like that in the whole of Hastings. It was a pocket compass in a little round case with a glass top. Even Charlie Lane's own father had said that he wished it belonged to him. When a person looked at that compass, he was fascinated — that's what he was, fascinated. Even Tom, who had owned that compass for years, could never look at it without secretly wondering what made the needle always point to the north. You couldn't get lost in the woods while you had that compass. Instead, you could be an explorer, exploring trackless wilds.

The sight of that treasure in Tom's hand made Charlie Lane almost burst with envy. He had wanted that compass for years. But he had never been able to talk Tom into a trade — never!

Charlie Lane was a smart boy. He saw through Tom's little game. The compass for a ride! Now was his chance. He looked around. No one in sight!

"All right, smarty!" he called, just as Tom really began to run. "Give me the compass, and you can have a ride."

"One ride for a compass like this!" Tom called back, beginning to sense victory. "What do you think I am?"

Charlie hesitated, but not for long. His desire for that compass was growing stronger with each passing minute. "How many then?" he shouted.

"A dozen!" announced Tom, stopping in his tracks and looking backward.

"A dozen! Why don't you ask me to give you the bicycle?" scoffed Charlie.

"Suit yourself," Tom called back, getting under way once more.

Now, Charlie knew Tom of old. You could go just so far with Tom. Charlie had visions of the compass' disappearing forever. "Make it half a dozen, and it's a bargain," he called in desperation.

Half a dozen! That was just the bargain Tom had hoped to drive. Six rides on a bicycle! Talk about adventure! Talk about success!

"All right!" he agreed doubtfully, as if he were not too well pleased. "But I'll keep the compass in my pocket until the rides are over."

There the matter ended. Another minute and Tom was wobbling uncertainly down a stretch of wooden sidewalk. His feet almost reached the pedals, but not quite. Yet the wobbles didn't last long. You know how a duck takes to water. Well, that's how Tom took to that bicycle.

And oh, the glorious feel of it! The thrill of being perched high in the air, astraddle the big wheel! The steady up-and-down pull of his feet on the pedals! The hollow, "woodeny" rattle of the loose planks beneath him! And the onward roll, roll, roll of the wheels carrying him forward!

"Isn't it grand?" shouted Charlie, running along beside him. "Say now, isn't it grand?"

    POCKET COMPASSES

It was too bad that the boys became so deeply interested in those rides that they forgot other things equally important. Five times Charlie helped Tom up or down steps or across street corners. Tom started bravely off on his last ride, and neither boy realized that each ride had brought them both farther back into town. Neither boy realized that they were both heading straight for trouble, until Charlie's little brother came bursting through a gate, shouting at the top of his voice,

"I'm going to tell Uncle John on you! Wait until he hears that Tom Hastings has been riding his bicycle! You just wait!"

Words can't tell how Charlie felt then. If you have ever been in a predicament like that, you know without telling. For a moment Charlie acted as though he were frozen, even though it was a sizzling, hot July day. He might have vented his temper upon his little brother and shouted, "I'll fix you if you tell!" But he didn't. Instead, he vented his temper upon Tom.

"Now see what you've done," he snapped. "Give me that compass, and give it to me quick. Then clear out! Never come near me again!"

All the rest of the day Charlie wouldn't let anyone come within ten feet of the bicycle. He did a splendid job of "locking the barn door after the horse was stolen." Unfortunately, Uncle John was a man of his word, even if he were a dandy. Prince Charlie's bicycle-riding days were over.

As for Tom, he never realized how much he treasured that compass until it was his no longer. Now he didn't have a thing that was different or better than the other boys had. Charlie paraded the compass all over town until even Grandmother heard about it. She sensed Tom's troubled feelings, but she said nothing, except to remark wisely,

"You enjoyed your bicycle rides, didn't you, Tom? Well, then, you'll have to be willing to pay the piper."

Tom didn't know what "pay the piper" meant, except that it was something very disagreeable.

"Horse Sense"

On the morning following the bicycle adventure, Jim Hastings was walking easily along, kicking up the sun-warmed dust of Maple Avenue on his way to Mr. Gray's barn. While he was kicking, he was carrying on a lively conversation with Ginger, his black-and-white pup, who was answering him with friendly leaps.

"They'll be glad to see us coming this time," Jim confided to Ginger, feeling of the pockets in his overalls. "I've a lump apiece for the rest of the horses and an extra lump for old Sobersides and the thoroughbred."

Ever since the morning before, Jim had had a guilty feeling. He had not meant to stop at Mr. Gray's barn when he joined the parade which followed the bicycle. Never before had he entered that barn empty-handed. He could still feel the soft, eager noses of the horses nuzzling away at his empty pockets. He could still hear their disappointed whinnies. Most clearly he could remember Sobersides, rolling her eyes until the whites showed and pawing the barn floor as if to say, "What! No sugar lump! What are you doing in this barn without my sugar lump?"

Sobersides was not a thoroughbred like Silver King. She was just an ordinary chestnut-brown colt, steadier than the other colts, with a determined way of her own. Of all the colts in Mr. Gray's barn, Jim liked her the best.

Jim Hastings was the only boy in town whom Mr. Gray would allow anywhere near his stable. Jim could be trusted not to frighten or tease the spirited horses and ruin them, perhaps, forever. He could be trusted to talk softly, to move quietly, to act gently, no matter what happened.

"Call it horse sense if you will," Mr. Gray used to say. "That Jim Hastings has a way with horses, a remarkable way for a boy who is only ten years old." A thrill of pride tingled up and down Jim's backbone whenever he heard this.

Now the boy and the dog turned in at the gate in the white picket fence and followed the long, dusty drive which led to the house. At some distance behind the house, atop a gently rising stretch of ground, could be seen the big gray barn. The morning sunlight was streaming through the wide-open doors. Here and there dark spots moved on the sunlit floor, as the hens wandered in or out, and the barn cats rose to stretch themselves in the sunlight.

Jim stopped for a moment to finish pumping a pail of water for Mrs. Gray from the pump at the kitchen door.

"You'll find the barn empty, Jim," Mrs. Gray remarked pleasantly, "and trouble enough around here for so early in the morning. We have always insisted that Tom Fuller was worth his weight in gold. But we never knew what we were talking about until this last month when Tom has been laid up with a broken leg. Not a man can we find to take his place in the barn. We have had four already, and not one of them worth his salt. Only this morning Mr. Gray caught the last one smoking a pipe as he went about his work."

"Smoking! In a barn! When he knew it wasn't allowed!" exclaimed Jim in astonishment.

"Smoking!" repeated Mrs. Gray. "When we haven't had rain for weeks, and everything is as dry as tinder!"

"What did Mr. Gray do about it?" asked Jim.

"Gave him his walking papers not ten minutes ago," announced Mrs. Gray, "and set off to find another man to take his place."

"If I were a man," said Jim decidedly, "I know whom he could get."

"So do I," smiled Mrs. Gray, "but you aren't. So run along and stay with the horses until Mr. Gray returns."

Jim had a habit of standing for a moment in the barn door, listening to the welcoming whinnies which greeted him on every side. Then he would move from one roomy stall to another, waiting long enough for the horses to begin nosing at his sleeve or nuzzling at his pockets before bringing forth his sugar lumps.

This morning, as he stood in the barn door, Jim had a queer feeling of something in the air — something that shouldn't be there. The horses were restless and uneasy. Perhaps they missed Tom Fuller more with each change of groom. Perhaps Mr. Gray had not been careful to hide the anger in his voice when he gave the last groom his walking

papers. Whatever it was, Jim knew that he must talk more softly and move more quietly than usual.

"Steady, Lady, steady," he said quietly, as he finished with Sobersides, gave her a playful slap, and moved on to the next stall. Lady pawed the barn floor nervously. She nipped at the boards of her stall as Jim reached for the sugar lump. Her nervous, excited whinny called forth answering whinnies from up and down the whole length of the barn.

"Something *is* wrong," thought Jim, looking about him, but discovering nothing different or unusual in the barn.

The restless, uneasy feeling began to take hold upon Jim, also. Again he looked about him. Suddenly he gave a quick start. The horse in the stall in front of him shied in fright. Now Jim knew! He *smelled* something! Through the open door at the end of the barn he *saw* something! *Smoke—* coming from the haymow above his head! *Fire—* in a haymow full of June hay!

Jim's first impulse was to yell *"Fire!"* but, fortunately for the horses, the cry would not come. For a moment he almost gave way to a wild desire to reach for the empty buckets in the barn door, to fill them at the horse trough behind the barn, and to dash up the ladder to the haymow. But Jim's "horse sense" kept him from doing anything so foolish.

Jim knew all about barn fires. Mr. Gray had warned him about them a thousand times. Another few minutes and that haymow would be a raging inferno. That's what Mr. Gray had said it would be — a raging inferno. Never try to save a barn. It simply can't be done. Get out the horses and save the water for the house and the rest of the outbuildings.

As these thoughts raced through Jim's head, another and more important thought came to take their places. Cover the horses' heads! Mr. Gray had told him never to forget that. He had read about it in a book, too — *Black Beauty*. You'd never get horses out if you didn't cover their heads. They wouldn't leave a burning barn. Jim looked quickly around. Grain sacks hanging on a nail! Sobersides first! No, he couldn't do that! Silver King, the thoroughbred, must be first.

HORSE TROUGH   HALTERS   BUCKETS

HORSE

COW

Jim could hardly control his shaking arms and legs as he threw the grain sack over Silver King's head. By this time the thoroughbred was thoroughly frightened. Jim had to climb on the bars of the box stall to keep out of the way of his prancing hoofs. "Will he leave the barn even now?" thought Jim, as he tied a rope to the ring of the halter and let down the bars of the stall. Fortunately for Jim, Silver King followed him.

Even before Jim reached the door, he saw Mrs. Gray coming in, white-faced, shaking, but quiet and self-controlled. She had not lived for years with a man who liked horses without knowing what to do when horses were in danger.

"Get them out if you can, Jim," she said quietly, "but watch out for yourself first. I'm going to the neighbors for help."

As Jim led Silver King into the open air, he caught sight of his cousin, Sam White, at the pasture gate. He left Silver King to Sam's care and closed the barn doors behind him. Horses will sometimes run back into a burning barn. He must take no chances with the thoroughbred.

Now Jim could hear the crackling sound of the fire, and in one place he could see flames shooting down between the boards above his head.

"Good for you, boy," he heard a quiet voice say, as he turned around after closing the doors. "Silver King, at least, is safe. Just happened to be passing when I saw the smoke! Leave the horses to me now. There will be plenty of help here in a minute. Jump into my buggy by the front gate and ride for dear life to the Town Hall and ring the fire bell. We'll do what we can until the engine gets here. Run along now! This is man's work!" It was Silas Johnson speaking, Mr. Gray's neighbor on the north.

Jim lingered long enough to see Sobersides leaving the barn. Then he made a beeline for the waiting buggy. All his pent-up feeling released itself in one wild cry of *"Fire!"* One cry — no more! What was he thinking of? Did he want to start a runaway? He reached for the reins thrown loosely over the hitching post, gave the horse a flick of the whip, and started down Maple Avenue at breakneck speed.

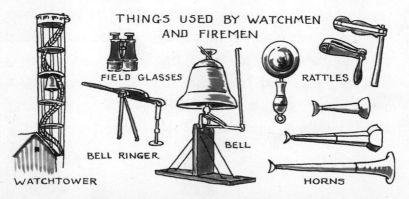

THINGS USED BY WATCHMEN AND FIREMEN

FIELD GLASSES

RATTLES

BELL RINGER

BELL

WATCHTOWER

HORNS

Young America

By this time everyone was running in the direction of the barn. Men and women with pails and buckets! Boys and girls yelling *"Fire!"* at the tops of their voices! Buggies raced by, going in the opposite direction from Jim and his speeding horse. In one of the buggies Jim saw the sober, anxious face of Mr. Gray.

"I'll ring the fire bell, Jim. I'll get there sooner than you can," called Silas Lane, passing Jim with his fast trotter on his way to town. "But follow me in case I have an upset!"

Even before Jim reached the foot of the Fox Street hill, he could hear the loud clang of the fire bell from the tower of the Town Hall on the island. Now Jim could see in his mind's eye just what was happening. All over town, in railroad shops, stores, and mills, men who belonged to the volunteer fire department had dropped their work like a flash and were making a mad dash for the Town Hall. Another minute and men would be rushing from all directions. Here came Joseph Palmer, the Fire Captain, out of Jim's father's store now. Jim pulled sharply on the reins, and Joseph Palmer jumped in beside him.

"Where's the fire, Jim? In John Gray's stable, you say? With those prize horses? Good land, boy, we'll be in luck if the hose on *Young America* reaches that far. We'll have to draw water from the river. There isn't a cistern with a drop of water in it in the whole of Hastings. Not after this dry spell! Here's hoping someone has begun to get up steam in that boiler."

Jim dashed through the covered bridge, then drew to a quick stop in front of the Town Hall on the island.

Even as Captain Palmer jumped from the buggy, six stalwart firemen came running from the fire barn in the rear of the Town Hall, pulling the fire engine, *Young America*, by a heavy rope fastened to the front axle. Other firemen raced ahead with the two-wheeled hose cart.

Young America was a splendid engine, the most up-to-date engine that money could buy. Its big upright boiler was a brilliant red. The smoke-stack, the safety valve, and the rest of the fittings were of shining brass. On the side of the boiler was the steam gauge whose dancing needle showed when the pressure of the steam in the boiler was great enough to set the water pump going. Under the boiler was the firebox. At this moment a fireman stood on the platform at the back of the fire engine, facing the firebox, a box of chips on one side of him and a box of coal on the other. With his eye glued to the steam gauge, he was piling more chips and more coal into the firebox, where a fire had already been started.

As soon as the gathering company saw that there were hands enough to pull the engine, the rest of the firemen raced ahead in the direction of the fire at breakneck speed. Some of them were carrying the long fire ladders. Jim, turning his horse's head around and following the engine back through the covered bridge, found some of the firemen hopping in beside him.

Now the engine turned south on Broadway, the street which ran parallel with Maple Avenue on the hilltop to the east. It stopped at a point in

FIRE IMPLEMENTS

RATTLE AXES SPANNERS

line with Mr. Gray's barn. By this time Jim could see the smoke and flames towering above the trees and houses to the eastward.

On each side of *Young America's* boiler was a large brass pipe to the ends of which the long rolls of fire hose from the hose cart were quickly fastened. Two lengths of hose were carried down a side street to the river on the west, and the ends of the hose were dropped into the water. The other two lengths were carried up the same side street to the east in the direction of Mr. Gray's barn. The engine was pulled as far in the same direction as it was possible to go without pulling the ends of the first lengths from the water.

"Wasted effort, I tell you," Captain Palmer kept saying over and over, as the men worked in desperate haste. "This engine was meant only to protect the business district. Without a water supply nearer than the river, it can never pump a stream of water long enough to reach that barn. And there's not a cistern within a mile with a drop of water in it, into which we can drop the hose. Wasted effort, I tell you!"

Captain Palmer was right. Steam was up in the boiler. The suction pump worked with might and main, sucking water from the river through two lengths of hose and shooting it forth through the other two lengths in incredibly long streams of water. Incredibly long, but not long enough! Even when all the hose was combined into one long length, the stream of water did not reach Mr. Gray's gate, to say nothing of the house and the barn.

"Slow down the pump! We'll use the hose to fill the buckets, and we'll form a bucket brigade!" shouted Captain Palmer to the fireman who was tending the firebox.

Before many minutes two long lines of men extended from the end of the fire hose to Mr. Gray's barnyard. Jim, eager to do a man's work, was among them. Buckets of water were passed along one line of waiting men and up the ladders to the firemen on the house roof and on the roofs of the other outbuildings. The empty buckets were passed back along the second line of waiting men to the fire hose. Slow work and seemingly hopeless on account of its slowness! Yet only if the walls and roofs were well-soaked, was there any chance of saving the other buildings from catching on

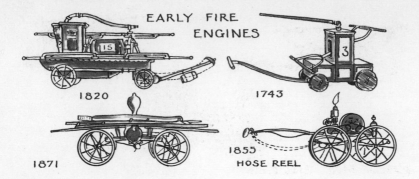

EARLY FIRE ENGINES

1820

1743

1871

1855
HOSE REEL

fire from the flying sparks and cinders from the great barn. Another bucket brigade leading from Mr. Gray's own well helped in the fight. In this brigade Tom and Charlie worked side by side, their differences of the day before all forgotten.

The heat of the day plus the terrific heat from the burning barn caused many men to fall exhausted. Once, in the midst of the fight, Jim felt a hand on his shoulder. He looked up into the soot-blackened face and bloodshot eyes of Mr. Gray. "I always said you had horse sense, lad," said Mr. Gray soberly. That was the only thing he said to Jim about the fire that day; but it was praise enough, and Jim never forgot it.

All morning the fight went on. All that day and the next men kept close watch upon the smoldering ruins. As to the cause of the fire, everyone seemed to agree. "All for the sake of a pipe of tobacco," remarked Mr. Gray bitterly.

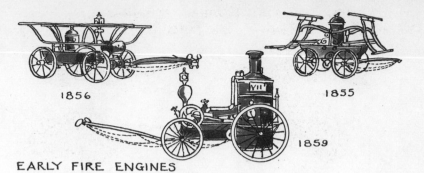

1856

1855

1859

EARLY FIRE ENGINES

In the days following the fire, men went about Hastings sober-faced and thoughtful. "Only a piece of good luck kept it from being your barn or mine," one man would say to another.

There were those shortsighted ones who, in the excitement of the moment, blamed the engine. "All the town's money sunk in a newfangled engine that can't do the job!" they exclaimed in disgust.

"Come, now," argued Mayor Hastings in his easy, quiet way. "There isn't a better engine in the land, but we didn't bargain for an engine which could furnish its own water supply, did we? What this town needs is a water system — wells drilled so deep that they will never run dry, and a standpipe high enough to give us the pressure we need, in which to store the water. We need water mains running under the streets we are standing on to carry the water where we want it to go. Think that over, gentlemen! Remember, think it over!"

Great Plans

Days went by, and people did think over what the mayor had said. Indeed, by the end of the week many people were talking of the water system as if it were their own original idea.

"There isn't a second to lose," insisted Jim, as he rode about town in the yellow wagon with the little fat butcher. "We must have fire protection,

Captain Palmer says. The only thing which saved us this time is the fact that there wasn't a breath of air stirring. Another fire like the last one, with a good stiff breeze blowing, and the whole town will go up in smoke."

"How have we lived in this town all these years and allowed it to get so far behind the times?" exclaimed Samuel White, the owner of the newspaper. He was standing with his wife on the front veranda, looking in despair at a long stretch of burned lawn and dried-up flower beds. "I can't ask Sam to pump water from a well to keep a lawn green in a summer like this. Now, if we had what we should have — garden hose and a plentiful supply of water piped to our own doors — Hastings would be a different-looking place. Didn't I say five years ago that we needed a water system?"

"Water system! Poppycock!" exploded Dan Cutter over the counter in his cigar store. "A newfangled idea that will cost money! Hastings has got along without a water system in the past, and it can do so in the future! Poppycock, I say!"

"I declare! I never start work that I don't find the water pail empty!" complained good-natured Norah in Banker Hastings' kitchen. "I look about for that boy, and the bird has flown.

Dragging water day and night will be the death of me. And to think that if this were an up-to-date town, I could get water from a faucet on the wall!"

"Here I am, building a new house in an old-fashioned way!" thought Joseph White in disgust, as he stood in front of his new house on Elm Street. "Of course I should have running water upstairs and down, and a bathtub to make life easier and more pleasant. In a town without water mains, I can have neither the one nor the other."

"This water isn't fit to drink!" said Mrs. Lane to her husband, as they watched Charlie pump and pump to get one pail of water from an almost-dry well. "I heard yesterday that six children on Pigeon Hill were sick from drinking water from a well like this. Are we never to have pure drinking water in this town? Are we to wait until we are all sick and it is too late?"

"Not if I can help it," replied Mr. Lane, with a determined set to his chin. "Water from this well is safe no longer. It must be boiled, and one thing is certain. Hastings must stop talking and *do* something about its water supply."

But "doing something" was a big undertaking, as Mr. Lane soon found out. Wells, deep enough to give Hastings the supply of pure water it needed,

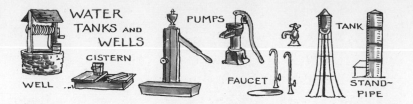

WATER TANKS AND WELLS

WELL   CISTERN   PUMPS   FAUCET   TANK   STAND-PIPE

must be drilled deep down through underground rock. One such well would cost thousands of dollars. Thousands more would be needed to build a standpipe in which to store the water, and still more thousands to lay the iron pipes of the water mains five feet below street level to carry the water to all parts of town. Where was the money to come from?

"It will take planning, I admit," said Mayor Hastings thoughtfully. "But in a matter as important as this, Hastings must find a way out."

And Hastings did find a way out. There were men, both in town and the country round, who had money for which they had no present use. They were willing to lend the money to the town of Hastings so that the work of putting in the water system could begin at once, provided that in return they were given certain papers called bonds. These bonds were promises from the town to repay the money after a certain number of years. Until such time as the money was repaid, each man must be paid six cents a year for every dollar lent. This six cents was called interest.

Before lending any money, these men had to be sure of two things. Would the town be able to pay the interest year after year? Would there be funds enough on hand to pay back the borrowed money when the time came to do so?

"The interest needn't worry you," said the mayor. "Once water is piped into the houses, each family will pay a small yearly fee for the water used. The water fees will pay the interest."

How Hastings was to accumulate thousands of dollars to pay back the borrowed money when the

time came to do so was another matter. Days and weeks of thought and planning showed that there was only one way out. Every man in Hastings who owned a house and lot, a store building, or even a vacant lot paid taxes each year on the property he owned. The money coming in from property taxes was used to pay the expenses of running the town. If, for every dollar of property tax now paid each year, property owners would be willing, instead, to pay one dollar and ten cents, wells and water mains would be possible. The extra tax money coming in could be put into the bank to accumulate over the years. In ten years there would be enough on hand to pay off half the bonds. In twenty years there would be enough to pay off the rest.

In the end, an election was called to find out what the voters of Hastings thought about the matter and to give them a chance to vote "yes" or "no" on two questions. Should Hastings have a water system? Should the town borrow the money necessary to make a water system possible? Every property owner who voted "yes" to these two questions knew that he was raising his own taxes. Some men like Mr. Cutter voted "no." But most of the voters agreed with Mr. Lake.

"'Twill raise my taxes five dollars a year, but it's worth it," said Mr. Lake with conviction. "Think what I'll get for my money! Fire protection, pure drinking water, and some comforts in life for my wife and family!"

Since most of the voters voted "yes," the rest of the voters had to agree. All property owners must pay the extra property tax, and Hastings was to have a water system. Plans went forward immediately, and summer was scarcely over before well drilling was under way.

Now Tom, looking for excitement, no longer stopped on Pigeon Hill. He followed the rest of

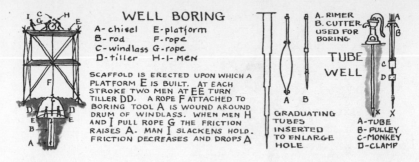

WELL BORING

A- chisel   E- platform
B- rod   F- rope
C- windlass   G- rope
D- tiller   H-I- MEN

SCAFFOLD IS ERECTED UPON WHICH A
PLATFORM E IS BUILT. AT EACH
STROKE TWO MEN AT EE TURN
TILLER DD. A ROPE F ATTACHED TO
BORING TOOL A IS WOUND AROUND
DRUM OF WINDLASS. WHEN MEN H
AND I PULL ROPE G THE FRICTION
RAISES A. MAN I SLACKENS HOLD.
FRICTION DECREASES AND DROPS A

A- RIMER
B- CUTTER
USED FOR
BORING

TUBE
WELL

GRADUATING
TUBES
INSERTED
TO ENLARGE
HOLE

A- TUBE
B- PULLEY
C- MONKEY
D- CLAMP

the boys to a place on the riverbank where land had been bought for a well site. Across the road was a high knoll where the standpipe was to be. There were always men about the well site, talking in groups, and the boys liked to listen.

Elsewhere in Hastings the girls and the house-wives were atingle with other ideas.

"Mama is planning a bathroom at the end of our upstairs hall," Mary Hastings confided to her cousin, Sally White. "Did you ever see a real bathtub, Sally? Mama says it is made out of tin with wood all around the edges."

"No," said Sally, "I've never seen one, but I've seen a picture of one. It was big enough to drown in, if you weren't careful. Imagine taking a bath upstairs, and not in a wooden washtub in front of the kitchen stove!"

So the talk and the dreams and the plans went on; and while summer days passed quickly by, other important things were happening in Hastings.

White Mail

Tom and his cousin, Sam White, with fish poles over their shoulders, came racing down the New York Street hill on their way to Frogtown to go fishing.

"It's almost time for the White Mail! Let's wait!" shouted Tom, as they reached the foot of the hill. The boys stopped with a suddenness which almost sent them sprawling in the dust in front of the watchman's shanty by the railroad tracks. Another minute and they were poking their noses in at the door of the shanty where Old Joe and Big Jack Casey, the best policeman in Hastings, were enjoying an argument.

"It's a law we need, and a fine for those who won't obey it," thundered Big Jack, waving his billy from his seat on the nail keg in the corner. "Do you know where I found your Buttercup this morning? Munching grass in front of 'The House on the Hill'! An ordinary cow from Pigeon Hill eating the mayor's grass!"

"And why not?" retorted Old Joe, in danger at any minute of slipping through the big hole in his cane-seated chair. He laid aside his red flag,

the better to slap his good knee and talk about the rights of the poor man. "To whom do the streets of this town belong, I ask you? To the people of Hastings! And whose grass are those cows eating and changing into good milk? Our grass, I tell you!"

The boys slipped quietly in and perched on top of the rusty iron stove. Even then the arguing didn't stop, not for a single second. Tom gave Sam a poke in the ribs and grinned a broad grin. Sam poked and grinned in return. Nothing was more fun than listening to Big Jack and Old Joe when they once got started. No one would think, to hear them go on, that there weren't two better friends in the whole of Hastings.

"Our grass, your grass, you say!" scoffed Big Jack, in answer to Old Joe's last words. "Stuff and nonsense! That one-horned cow of yours won't eat grass. She can open any garden gate in Hastings. That's what she does! Opens the gates and invites in all her friends!"

"And isn't her milk the sweeter for eating flowers instead of wayside grass?" replied Old Joe, chuckling with laughter.

"If it's sweeter milk she gives, I'll be tasting it to find out," retorted Big Jack, grinning in spite of himself as he bent down his head to get through the door. "I'll be locking her up in my own barn the next time I catch her roaming. Don't forget that!"

"He will, too," said Old Joe, with a doubtful headshake in the boys' direction. "So keep a good eye on my Buttercup! And now what can I do for you two? You weren't figuring on fishing out of my shanty window, were you?"

"We're waiting for the White Mail, and here she comes!" cried Sam, jumping down from his seat on the stove and hurrying for the door. From not too far away came the toot of an engine whistle and the sound of an engine bell. Tom and Old Joe didn't budge an inch.

"You'll never make a railroad man until you sharpen your ears," said Old Joe, with a look of annoyance in Sam's direction. "Tell him, son," he said then, turning to Tom.

"It's Number 20, switching in the yards," announced Tom confidently, without even glancing toward the door or window.

"Right!" declared Old Joe, his look of annoyance changing to a smile of pleased satisfaction. "You're after my own heart, lad. You know your engine bells when you hear them."

"How could you tell? How could you, without even looking?" exclaimed Sam, staring at Tom in surprise and consternation.

"He has an ear for the tone of the bell, lad," explained Old Joe. "Every engine bell has its own particular tone. Some bells have more silver in them, and some have less. But every good engine bell these days has some, and no two bells have the same amount. It's the silver that makes the difference. Prick up your ears and make a business of listening, and you'll grow smarter as you grow older."

"Number 12! Here she comes now!" announced Tom with equal confidence, as another engine bell sounded from the distance.

Almost before the words were out of Tom's mouth, Old Joe, flag in hand, was turning the handle and letting down the crossing gates. Down the tracks, slowing to a stop, came Number 12, and behind the engine and the tender came the United States Mail car all painted white.

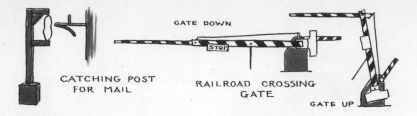

CATCHING POST FOR MAIL

GATE DOWN

RAILROAD CROSSING GATE

GATE UP

Tom and Sam raced across the street to the depot. There, sitting in state by the side of the track in his two-wheeled gig, sat Mr. Chase, the postmaster of Hastings. He had locked the post office for the time being, to drive down and pick up the mail. The boys were just in time to see a mail sack fly from the door of the mail car and land on the seat beside him. At the same moment a second sack flew from Mr. Chase's hands into the hands of a grinning mail clerk. Through the open door, the boys caught glimpses of the same clerk sorting letters into pigeonholes along the walls of the car.

Minutes passed while larger packages were loaded into the Railway Express car directly behind the White Mail. Then, with two blasts of the engine whistle and the loud ringing of the bell, the White Mail was again under way.

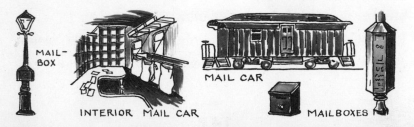

MAIL-BOX

INTERIOR MAIL CAR

MAIL CAR

MAILBOXES

Frogtown

Immediately Tom and Sam remembered that they were going fishing. They rescued their fish poles from the shanty and raced down Broadway.

"Let's walk the trestles," dared Sam, hurrying past the turn which would take them across the covered bridges at Fox Street, and continuing on his way south.

"Let's! It's safe!" said Tom with conviction. "There won't be another train through here for hours."

"Good thing there isn't a bridgetender on this bridge," said Sam a few minutes later, as the boys started gingerly across the railroad bridge to the west bank of the Big Turtle. "He'd never let us try this."

The wooden trestles felt blistering hot to their bare feet under the burning heat of the midsummer sun. Down below them lay Round Island with yellowing willow trees bending over the stony river bed round its edges. The grass in the center of the island had long since burned to a deep reddish brown in the dead mid-August heat.

Once the bridge was behind them, the boys came to the low, flat bottom lands along the west

bank of the Big Turtle. "Frogtown"—that's what
people called this part of town, and you didn't live
here if you wanted to sleep nights.

The boys followed the rocky path by the water's
edge. Down where the willows followed the bend
in the shore, where the mosquitoes and frogs were
thickest, there was the best fishing hole on the
river, that is, if any place could be a good fishing
place in such a summer.

Now, as they turned the bend in the shore, the boys stopped for a moment to examine their cans of worms. Worms were hard to get in this weather, and it was good sense to keep an eye on them.

As they looked up again, they saw someone — a boy — sitting with his back against a tree. His fish pole was propped up against the low branch of a willow tree, and his head was buried — of all places — in a book.

"It's Jim," whispered Sam, so overcome with astonishment that he couldn't talk out loud. "Look, Tom, look! He's got a bite on his hook, and he doesn't even know it!"

"He doesn't even hear us coming!" grunted Tom in disgust. "Listen to him! He's laughing to himself! He's laughing over an old book!"

"Hello, Jim! What're you doing?" called Sam the next minute.

Jim broke into a loud chuckle, but he didn't even glance up.

"He's gone crazy!" grunted Tom. "Look! The mosquitoes are eating him up, and he doesn't even give them a whack!" Tom's disgust grew and grew. "What do you think you are?" he called loudly. "A professor?"

Now Jim came to life. He looked up, his eyes alight with eager excitement. "Do you want to know how to fetch a wart?" he asked breathlessly. "A sure way? Listen to this!"

You take your dead cat and go and get in the graveyard 'long about midnight where somebody that was wicked has been buried: and when it's midnight a devil will come, or maybe two or three, but you can't see 'em, you can only hear something like the wind, or maybe hear 'em talk: and when they're taking the feller away, you heave your cat after 'em and say, "Devil follow corpse, cat follow devil, warts follow cat. I'm done with ye!" That'll fetch any wart.

For one instant Tom stood "dumbstruck," staring at Jim. The next, he made a wild but unsuccessful grab for the book. "Where did you get that? Let's see! Let's see!"

Instantly there were three heads in a huddle. In the center of the huddle was a book in a blue-cloth cover with decorations of black and gold. It would have taken sharp eyes to figure out who was saying what for the next few minutes.

"Where'd you get it?"

"My father gave it to me."

"Where'd he get it?"

"A man came to our house peddling! A little man with lots of hair! Clemens — that's his name. He wrote this book."

"Huh! He did not! It says right here! *The Adventures of Tom Sawyer* by Mark Twain."

"He did too write it! He said so! Mark Twain is just the name he took. 'Mark Twain' means two fathoms deep. Those are just some words the boatmen on a river use when they're measuring how deep the water is."

"Mississippi! That's the river! It says so on this page. He was smart to think up that name!"

"Where does it say that about the dead cat and the warts?"

"I'll show you! My father says he was ashamed of himself the way he laughed over this book. He got a hundred laughs for every cent he put into it."

"And the boy's name's Tom!"

"Yes, and wait till you hear how he whitewashed the fence, and how he saw an Indian kill a man in the dead of night by the light of the moon!"

Minutes passed. The fish still hung unnoticed

on Jim's hook, and worms crawled from overturned cans on the riverbank. Three pairs of eyes fairly flew over the pages as Jim pointed out the good parts with an "Oh, stop! Wait a minute! I forgot to read this!"

Jim had just read the part where Tom Sawyer came secretly home in time for his own funeral, when men's voices in interested discussion sounded from around the bend in the shore of the Big Turtle. Another minute and there were the Mayor of Hastings; Mr. Joseph White, the owner of the Hastings brickyard; Mr. Thomas Hastings, the banker; Mr. Silas Lane, the miller; and several other well-known men of Hastings. With them were three or four strangers. What in the world were they doing in Frogtown in the middle of the morning? Truly this was a day when things seemed to be happening and happening and happening!

Something important was under way. That much was certain. Not one of the men spoke to the boys as he passed by. Even Grandfather only recognized them with a nod of his head. If you want to make a boy curious, pass him by without speaking. *Tom Sawyer's* covers closed with a bang, and the three boys trailed along at Grandfather's heels, far enough behind to keep out of trouble but close enough to hear what was going on.

"A splendid place for coke ovens!" Silas Lane was saying. "This land has never been good for much. I've talked to the man who owns it, and we can get it for a song."

"The railroad can run a track from the end of the bridge and switch loaded coal cars right up to our door!" added Banker Hastings.

"That island in the river! How about that?" asked one of the strangers. "Just the place for the holder, in my way of thinking!"

"A good idea," replied the mayor. "Then, if by any chance it catches on fire, there will be the river on all sides to protect the town."

CANDLES   OIL   GAS

"That holder won't catch on fire! Don't worry about that!" answered the stranger. "Is there any reason why the pipes can't be carried above water across the river?"

On and on and on went the talk. Some of it the boys understood, but most of it they didn't. By and by an idea began to dawn upon them. Why — these men were talking about *gas!* Gas to light the streets of Hastings! Gas to light the houses! They were going to manufacture that gas right here on this riverbank!

"Whoo-pee!" Tom almost shouted. "Wait till Mary hears about this!" Then he caught himself in time and lowered his voice to a whisper. "How she hates to wash lamp chimneys!"

"We don't want gas in this town! It's dangerous!" whispered Jim excitedly. "I know because I saw gaslights in the city when I stayed at the hotel. The gas came out of the end of a pipe, and you lighted the end of the pipe. There was a little handle by which you could turn the gas on and

off. Over every gas jet there was a big sign —
DON'T BLOW OUT THE LIGHT! Every man
in the hotel told you the same thing — DON'T
BLOW OUT THE LIGHT! TURN IT OUT!
Do you know what would happen if you blew out
the light and went to bed? You'd be dead by
morning! And you wouldn't even know you were
dying! What do you know about that?"

"I'd rather have an old candle," said Sam.

"Yes, but maybe we'd have fun going round with the lamplighter," Jim went on. "You see, they put the gas lamps for the streets up on tall iron poles. Then every evening the lamplighter comes round with a little short ladder and a lighted taper."

"And climbs the ladder, and turns on the gas, and lights the lantern!" Tom broke in. "And what do you bet! I'll be doing it, too!"

Now the talk was coming to an end, and the men stood together in a group on the riverbank.

"Well, gentlemen," said the most important-looking stranger, "there is nothing more to be said. Enough of you men have put money into this company to make it safe to start. The State has given us our charter. We stand ready to pay the Town Council of Hastings the fee they ask for the right to operate a gas company in this town. All there is left to do at present is to settle the matter of buying this land. Let's be about it!"

The boys were bursting with news as they raced back over the Fox Street bridges into town. They hadn't an idea in their heads what a charter was. They hadn't an idea what the holder was, either, which was to be built on the island in the river.

They had never heard the word "coke" before in all their lives. But you don't have to know all there is to know about anything before you spread the news. Some things can wait.

"Gas!" exclaimed Mr. Cutter, laying down the feather duster with which he was dusting the cigar-store Indian. "I've no intention of blowing up my store. I've been saying for a year that if gas will burn when it comes out of a pipe, why won't it burn in a pipe? I've no desire to see pipes full of fire running under the streets I'm walking over. No gas for me! I'm against it!"

"Gas!" exclaimed Mr. Hunt, moving his old rocker to the shady side of the livery stable. "Good news! So the plan has gone through! I'll put money into that venture myself. This town is as dark as a pocket the minute the sun goes down. Anything could have happened on these streets after dark through all these years. We're fortunate that nothing terrible did happen. Now we can walk around at night and know where we're going."

"Gas!" exclaimed Mr. Fields, as he mounted the steps of the Field House. "No gas in this hotel! I've worries enough without having to turn out lights for forgetful people who can't remember that they're killing themselves."

"Ha, ha! That reminds me!" laughed Mr. Brooks from his seat on the Field House veranda. "Come here, boys! I'll sing you a song! A good song I heard in the city!"

In another few minutes the boys were swinging their heels from the veranda railing as they joined in the singing with might and main. It was surprising the speed with which they learned that song!

> "A man who lived a long way off
>   Came in to see the town,
>   He spent the night at Field's Hotel,
>   And said his name was Brown.

> "He went upstairs to go to bed,
>   He was as green as grass,
>   Took off his clothes, jumped into bed,
>   And then blew out the gas.

> "Oh, Mr. Brown, poor Mr. Brown,
>   We'll never see him more,
>   Until we meet again some day,
>   On the faraway, beautiful shore."

"Faraway shore! That's heaven! That means he's dead!" exclaimed Sam, stopping his singing long enough to explain.

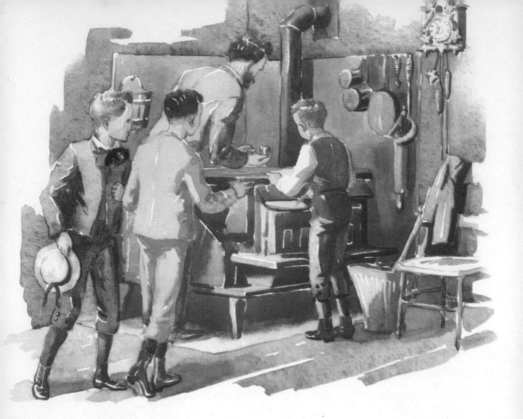

All the rest of the day the boys sang that song.
They hummed it, they whistled it, they played
it on their mouth organs. They even tried it on
the jew's-harp. They taught it to every boy and
girl who would stand still long enough to learn.
Sam and Tom were still singing it when thoughts
of a blue-covered book carried them over to Jim's
house that evening. There they found Jim and
his father, bending over a cookstove in a sizzling
hot kitchen, busy with an old clay pipe.

"Look! We're manufacturing gas! We'll have some before long!" Jim declared eagerly. "We put a piece of soft coal into the bowl of this pipe. Now we've sealed the top of the bowl tight shut with clay. Here, Sam, blow on this pipestem. Don't blow hard."

Sam's cheeks began to puff out, but no air came from the pipe bowl.

"It's airtight! Now we're ready!" declared Jim.

With the help of long-handled pincers, Jim held the pipe down among the hot embers. After a time, the coal in the pipe bowl became white-hot. The boys could not see it inside the bowl, but that's what Jim's father said it became — white-hot. Gas began to come from the pipestem; and when Jim lighted a match and held it to the pipestem, the gas burned. It actually burned.

"That's how it is, boys," said Jim's father, as they sat under the sugar maple in the back yard to cool off. He dug the clay from the top of the pipe bowl, and there in the bottom of the bowl was something which looked a little like soot and a little like coal.

"Do you know what that is?" he asked. "If there were more of it, we'd call it coke. Coke is coal from which the gas has been taken.

"What we did here tonight in a small way is just what we'll do on the riverbank," Jim's father went on. "We are going to heat coal until it is white-hot in airtight containers called retorts. When we're through, we'll have coke and gas. We'll have to do a good many things to that gas to purify it, to take out certain things which keep it from burning well. But we'll do it; and when we're through, we'll store the gas in a big iron tank on Round Island. That's what we mean when we talk about the holder — the big gas tank."

"The coke — what will you do with that?" asked Sam.

"Sell it to mills and factories to burn in place of coal," answered Mr. Hastings.

"Then you'll run gas mains under all the streets," announced Jim wisely, "and pipes up the lampposts and into the stores and houses. There'll be gas in every pipe. You'll put a cap on the end of each pipe with a slit to let the gas through. Then, when you turn on the gas and light it, there you'll be. This town will be as light as day. Even in the dead of night, it can be as light as day."

"Yes, and what will you do when the gas in the pipes gets on fire the way Mr. Cutter said it would?

What'll you do then?" asked Tom. "You'll blow up the streets and the whole town, too."

"Oh, no, we won't!" laughed Mr. Hastings. "Gas won't burn without air, Tom. There won't be any air in our retorts; there won't be any air in our holder; and there won't be any air in our pipes. We'll see to that. When the gas comes from the pipes and mixes with air, then it will burn, but not before."

"I bet you can't make Mr. Cutter believe that," declared Tom. "I bet you can't."

"I don't believe we'll try," laughed Mr. Hastings. "We'll wait until everyone else is burning gas. Then we'll let him find it out all by himself."

Any other night the boys would have sat under the maple tree for just so long. Then they would have been off and away, racing all over town, playing run sheep run or hunt the red fox. Tonight was different. They raced for the sitting room of Jim's house. They sat about the center table and

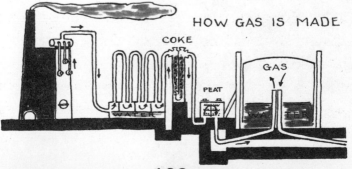

HOW GAS IS MADE

COKE

PEAT

GAS

WATER

WATER

pulled down the big hanging lamp which hung above it. They turned up the round wick until it smoked the lamp chimney. Then they lost themselves in a little blue book.

Jim's mother, coming in from rocking and fanning herself on the front veranda, found them there. She sent Tom and Sam "skedaddling." "Land sakes!" she cried all aflutter. "It's nine o'clock! Time for your fathers to be winding the clocks, and time for all folks to be in bed!"

As Jim mounted the stairs, there was a queer-looking lump inside his shirt. The hand in his pocket kept tight hold of a bit of candle and a match. He waited until his mother was asleep and his father was snoring. Then Jim found out for sure how Huckleberry Finn saved the widow.

Information, Please

From that time on, some part of each day found the boys in Frogtown, keeping an eye on the big brick retort house which was already being built.

"Why did anyone want to build a gas plant in this old place?" demanded Sam one morning, as he walked through the weeds and whacked away at the mosquitoes. "No one said a word about putting the water tank in Frogtown."

Mr. Joseph White, who was overseeing the unloading of bricks from his brickyard, happened to overhear him.

"Of course no one did," he said with an amused grin. "You see, Sam, things work this way. Water won't rise unless you force it to rise. When you build a standpipe, you build it on high ground and raise your tank high in the air. When the outlet to the tank is opened, the water rushes down with enough force to help lift the water in the mains and pipes as high as the upper stories of houses and store buildings. That same force helps to shoot long streams of water from the ends of fire hose. Gas, on the other hand, is very light. It needs no force to make it rise. It goes up more easily than it goes down. So when you build a gas tank, the best site is the lowest land in town. That's why we chose Round Island and the bottom lands along the river."

It was surprising the amount of information the boys picked up during the next few weeks.

"You see," explained wise Tom to Engineer Bill, "it's this way. No man in this town has money enough to build a gas plant all by himself. No man in any town has money enough for that. So a group of men get together and form a company."

"Yes, I know," said Big Bill. "Each man agrees to put in as much money as he can afford. He gets other men to join until the company has as much money as is needed. But even then it isn't a real company. Don't ever believe that."

"It isn't! Why not?" exclaimed Tom.

"Men can't form a company just because they want to," explained Big Bill. "Some companies might do things for their own good but not for the good of the people, such as charging too much for gas. Men can't form a company unless the State Government says so. The State has to give them a charter. That's a paper which says that it's all right to go ahead with the plans."

"This company *has* a charter," insisted Tom.

"No doubt it has," replied Engineer Bill.

A few days later Jim, on an errand to his grandfather's office, saw the famous charter.

"Here it is, son," said Mayor Hastings, as Jim leaned over his shoulder. "Our charter from the State Government! It gives us the right to manufacture and sell gas to be used for lighting streets and buildings. We can lay mains and pipes in any street or lane, and no other company can supply gas to Hastings for ten years to come. This is a mighty important paper!"

Late that same afternoon Sam poked his nose in at the door of the barn, where Tom was grumbling and milking the family cow.

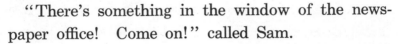

"There's something in the window of the newspaper office! Come on!" called Sam.

"Something in the window! What is it?" demanded Tom, as soon as the cow was milked and he could race after Sam down the street.

"Smarty! Don't you wish you knew?" teased Sam.

There in the window was an iron box with little dials on the outside. Each dial had a hand like the big hand on a clock. For once in his life, Tom was mystified. "What is that thing?" he demanded.

"You'll have one hanging on your cellar wall before next summer," grinned Sam. "It's a meter for measuring gas. All the gas that goes into your house will be piped through a meter like that. The meter will tell how much gas you use, down to the last foot. Then your father will have to pay. Every month he'll have to pay — three dollars for a thousand feet."

These were strange days. Now when a boy started to brag about his father, he didn't say, "My father's the smartest man in this town!" or, "My father can beat yours in a fight!" Instead he said, with thumbs under suspenders and fingers waving, "My father belongs to the gas company!"

The day when Jack Clancy from Pigeon Hill retorted, "Huh, you're not so important! My father does, too!" Tom and Charlie and Jack got into a terrible fight. They came home with bloody noses and torn shirts, much the worse for wear.

That night Tom's father got Tom and Charlie and sat them down on the bottom step of the front veranda. "If you're going around this town fighting and telling wild tales," he said, "you'd better know what you're talking about. Now listen, and don't let this go in one ear and out the other!

"Jack Clancy is right! His father does belong to the gas company. Your father, Charlie, and yours, Tom, are not the only men in this town. Every man who puts twenty-five dollars into the gas company has a share in the company. That means that he will get his share of the money we will make selling gas. He is a shareholder — stockholder, we sometimes call him. If he puts in two hundred fifty dollars, he owns ten shares; and he has a paper to prove that he owns ten shares. Not every company charges twenty-five dollars for its shares, but our charter says that that is what our shares are to sell for.

"At the end of the year we will pay the debts the company is supposed to pay that year. Then we will put some money aside — a sinking fund, we call it — to take care of unexpected expenses and other things which may come up during the next year. After that, the money left over will be divided among the shareholders. If we make a great deal of money, each shareholder will get a great deal. If we make only a little — well, I'll let you figure that out for yourselves. And the man who owns twenty-five shares will get twenty-five times as much as the man who owns one."

"And what if you don't make any money? What then?" asked Tom.

"That well may happen!" smiled Banker Hastings. "That's the risk you take when you buy shares in a company. You may make a lot of money, and you may make nothing. It's the risk that makes it interesting."

Tom's father had eyes in his head. He had ears, too, but they weren't very sharp. Still, he finally did notice that the boys were growing uneasy and more uneasy. And no wonder! How could they listen when Ned Fisher was stretched out on the big branch of the maple tree by the gate, whistling like an old bobwhite.

"Run along," said Mr. Hastings, with a broad grin, when he finally "tumbled."

"You must be in a peck of trouble. What was your pa lecturing about?" asked Ned of Tom, as

GAUGE

GAS METER

METER
WITH PART
OF FRONT
REMOVED
SHOWING
BELLOWS.

they raced for Charlie Lane's barn to try out
Charlie's new pair of stilts.

"He wasn't lecturing! Honest!" replied Tom.

"Poke me in the nose and see what happens!
Poke me in the nose if you expect me to believe
that!" retorted Ned, doubling up his fists.

Tom knew better than to get into another fight.
So he didn't poke, and he didn't expect. He just
kept still.

Banker's Children

Mary Hastings in a blue coverall apron, with hair tightly rolled in rag curlers, stood by the kitchen table dreamily polishing a lamp chimney.

The bracket lamp on the wall beside her with the tin reflector behind it was brimful of kerosene. The chimney in her hand gleamed like sunlight on rippling water. Yet on she went in a day-dreamy way, polishing, polishing, polishing.

Suddenly Mary's head tilted high in the air. She looked down her nose with a very superior expression. Why in the world did she do that?

The rag curlers and the superior expression didn't mix well together. The next minute a very stiff little smile turned up the corners of her mouth. No wonder good-natured Norah, slipping a pan of biscuits into the oven, had to bite her lips to keep from laughing.

"Stop the nonsense, lass, before you drop that chimney," she said kindly but energetically. "It will be five hours yet before you have your picture taken."

Mary flushed to the tips of her ears. She laughed an embarrassed little giggle as she reached up to put the chimney back into place. Then in an instant she grew sober and excited.

"Tell me, Norah, did you ever see a castle in the old country?" she asked expectantly.

"Many a one," nodded Norah, as a pan of bread followed the biscuits into the oven.

"Did they have curving steps leading up to them, with flowers and statues and everything?"

"Maybe they did in their good days," answered truthful Norah. "But every one I saw was tumbling to pieces."

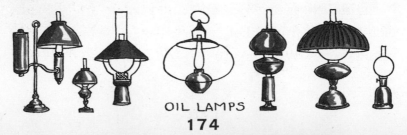

OIL LAMPS

"Mr. Reed has a screen like that in his photograph gallery," Mary hurried on. "Long, curving steps and a great window, just like a castle window! If I were to stand in front of a screen like that, I'd look as if I belonged to the castle, wouldn't I, Norah?"

"Ah, so there's where the dreams come in," nodded Norah, with a twinkle in her eye. "And why not, may I ask you? Who has a better right to belong to a castle than a lass like you?"

Mary thrilled with delight. Yet even as her eyes danced, her face fell.

"It will never be," she said mournfully. "You wait and see! Mama will prefer trees and mossy banks. Oh, Norah, why would anyone want to sit by a brook when he could belong to a castle? Why can't I do what I want to do — sometimes?"

"You can when you're grown-up, and you'll be grown-up a long time," comforted Norah. "Until then, do what you're told to do and do it with a smile, because you'll have to do it anyway. And now take your dreams and your fancies out of my kitchen before I burn my bread."

A minute or two later Mary was hurrying down the front walk. Castles had been forgotten for the moment in Mother's pleasant reminder that it was Mary's turn to pay the grocery bill. If you were a boy and paid the bill, Mr. Steel was sure to give you an apple for each hand. But if you were a girl, you got a red-and-green-striped bag of chocolate drops and sugar candy.

On the walk outside the gate several children were rolling hoops and racing along on roller skates. Instantly they spied the rag curlers.

"You're going away, aren't you?" they called over their shoulders. "Where are you going?" But they were gone before Mary could answer.

When Mary reached Mr. Steel's store, whom did she meet there, also paying a bill, but her cousin Sally. When Mr. Steel was through with

his teasing, the two girls walked home to Sally's house together, talking secrets and nibbling all the way. A few minutes later Sally's laughing voice could be heard calling, "You're dead on me!" A passer-by might have wondered what was going on, if he had not peered over the fence to see two pretty girls playing a game of croquet.

When noontime came round and Mary hurried home to set the table for dinner, she found things in a dreadful state. Mama was upstairs with Tom, washing his ears and scrubbing his neck and not being very gentle about it, either. Poor Tom, dragged home from roasting potatoes and frog legs down by Indian Creek, was so mad inside that he was red all over without any scrubbing.

"Ouch—you hurt—ouch!" he was yelling. Anyone would have thought he was being killed.

"Hurt, nothing!" exclaimed his mother. "Tom, Tom, how can you be so exasperating? Every family has to have its children's pictures taken once in a while. You knew this was coming, and you promised to behave. You know you did. So it won't do any good to raise a rumpus."

Mary grinned at Norah, and Norah winked at Mary. But they were both very careful to do their work well and to keep out of the way.

When Banker Hastings came home to dinner, there at the table sat a much-scrubbed, much-dressed-up Tom, hanging his head and looking as sour as ten days of bad weather. If Tom had glanced up, he would have known by the queer little twist at the corner of his father's mouth and by the amused twinkle in his father's eye that he, Tom Hastings, had one friend left in the world. But Tom didn't look up, and nothing in what his father said could lead anyone to believe that Mr. Hastings knew how it felt to give up roasting frog legs to have his picture taken.

"Now see here, Tom," said Mr. Hastings in a decided tone. "It is little enough to ask of you to give up an hour or two of fun to do something to please your mother. So take that look off your face and be quick about it, before I have to step in and settle the matter."

Tom did take the look off his face, but the one which replaced it was no improvement.

When Joe, the stableboy, drove the surrey up to the door that afternoon and Mrs. Hastings came out with Mary and Tom by her side, anyone would have been proud to claim a son and a daughter like that. Mary's new white dress had a looped over-skirt just like her mother's. Her ankle ties, her curls, her hat, and her tiny ruffled parasol were all in the latest fashion. Tom's long pants, his vest, his short buttoned-up coat made him look very grown-up. His hat sat on the top of his head at just the right angle. His high-buttoned shoes were as shiny as his face, and that was very shiny, indeed.

Joe stopped the surrey in front of a long, dark stairway on River Street. At the top of that stair-way was Mr. Reed's photograph gallery. It was a bare-looking room without much furniture and without even one window. All the light came from a skylight high overhead with shades to pull across instead of up and down.

Near the center of the room, on its three long legs, stood the camera all covered over with a black cloth. Close at hand were some long iron rods which moved up and down on standards. At the top of each rod was something which looked like half of a hoop. The hoops could be made wider or narrower to fit the back of a person's head. They were splendid things to hold your head still while your picture was being taken.

All around the four walls of the room were screens. Screens with purple clouds and fields painted upon them! Screens with woods and rippling brooks, and one screen "with long, curving steps and flowers and statues and everything"!

Over in one corner were a rock or two upon which you could sit by the brookside, and a bench and a piece of fence made out of logs. Then there was a dog, a sleek-looking plaster dog, sitting up on its haunches. The only real piece of furniture in the room was a beautiful carved chair with a very high back.

Mr. Reed was a fidgety little man with no hair at all, except a little over his ears.

"Shall we try the boy first?" he asked Mrs. Hastings. "Boys are harder! Or do you prefer the two together?"

"Not together," replied Mrs. Hastings. "And the boy first, by all means."

"The chair! I suggest the chair!" said Mr. Reed, buzzing about, placing the chair in just the right position, and pulling the shades back and forth across the skylight. In another minute Tom was standing with one hand on the chair back and the other stuck between the two middle buttons of his coat.

It was a beautiful chair, but all it did for Tom was to make him look longer and skinnier and stiffer than he had ever looked before. "Gangly," moaned Mrs. Hastings to herself. "That's how he looks—gangly!"

"Oh, dear! This will never do!" she said out loud. "Can't we try it sitting down?"

So Tom sat down. Now he didn't know what to do with the hand on the chair back. So he put it on his knee and spread out the fingers. Then it looked twice as big as a hand should look.

"Do something with it! Do something!" begged his mother. So Tom put his hand into his pocket.

"Oh, dear me! It will have to be a side view!" thought Mrs. Hastings the next minute. "His ears! I'm sure they never stuck out that way before. They've even grown bigger!"

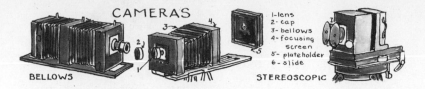

CAMERAS

BELLOWS STEREOSCOPIC

1- lens
2- cap
3- bellows
4- focusing
      screen
5- plateholder
6- slide

Mr. Reed stopped his fidgeting long enough to notice her worried expression. "Suppose we try the fence," he suggested hopefully. "The fence may suit him better."

So now Tom stood by the fence with a post to rest his hand upon. By his side was the sleek-looking plaster dog, the poorest excuse for a dog Tom had ever seen. He itched to reach out quickly with his foot and give it a kick, but he knew he had better behave and get this thing over with.

"Now we have it," said Mr. Reed airily. "A boy and his dog! 'Twill make a charming picture." Even Mrs. Hastings was satisfied.

Instantly Mr. Reed began darting in and out from under the black cloth over the camera, for all the world like a jumping jack. He turned Tom's head this way and darted back to take a look. He turned it that way and darted back to look again. At last he fastened it tight in the hoop. The rod and the hoop were behind Tom's back and didn't show from the front at all.

"Smile!" ordered Mr. Reed from under the cloth. Tom did his best. He even showed his back teeth.

183

Mr. Reed was scandalized. "Never show your teeth in a picture! Never!" he exploded, darting out once more to shake his bald head at Tom.

This time Tom just stretched his mouth, and everything went well.

"Hold still now—hold still!" insisted Mr. Reed, as he reached for the rubber bulb which hung down from the camera. One squeeze of the bulb, and the picture taking was over.

"Run along home, change your clothes, and be sure you're home in time for supper," gasped Mrs. Hastings with a sigh of relief. And Tom ran.

All this time Mary had been standing up so as not to wrinkle her dress. She had been acting

like a perfect lady. Mrs. Hastings had no idea
that she was in for more trouble.

"A country scene, I think," said Mrs. Hastings.
"Let her sit by the brook with her parasol over
her head and her hat on the ground beside her."

"Very well, madam! A charming girl, sitting
by the brookside! 'Twill make a lovely picture,"
beamed Mr. Reed, as he began to move the screens
about, looking for the right one.

"Oh, Mama," pleaded Mary, hurrying over to
the screen with the curving steps. "This is the one
I want! Please, Mama! Anyone can sit by a brook!"

"Why, Mary!" declared Mrs. Hastings. "What
an idea! That screen isn't suitable for a young
girl! Not suitable at all!"

"Oh, yes it is! Isn't it, Mr. Reed? It's the one I've been wanting to stand in front of forever and ever and ever." Mary looked disconsolate, absolutely disconsolate. Her eyes filled with tears which threatened at any minute to fall down upon her new white dress.

"Dear me!" thought Mrs. Hastings. "Now what?"

Under ordinary circumstances she would never have given in—*never!* But it was embarrassing to have her family act so in front of strangers. Mr. Reed would tell everyone all over town how the banker's children behaved. Anything to keep that from happening! She'd settle with Mary when she got her home. She certainly would!

But when Mary stood in front of the long, curving steps, she looked so lovely, and she stood so still, and she smiled such a completely happy smile, that Mr. Reed said she was the best young lady who had ever "sat" for a picture in his gallery. Then Mrs. Hastings almost forgave Mary, almost but not quite.

In about a week the pictures came. When Norah saw Mary in front of the long, curving steps, she declared that Mary looked exactly like a princess walking out of a castle. Grandmother agreed with Norah; and always after that, when Grandmother looked at the picture on the shelf above the fireplace in the parlor, she called it Princess Mary. And oh, was Mary thrilled!

As for Tom's picture, it was good enough. But somehow the smile didn't go with Tom, and Tom didn't go with the dog, and the dog didn't go with the fence. Anyway, there was something the matter. Tom's picture stood on the mantelshelf for a time, too, but one day Mr. Hastings found Tom's mother putting it away in the small, round-topped trunk where she kept her treasures.

"Cheer up, my dear," grinned Mr. Hastings. "Homely boys always make the best-looking men!"

"How you talk!" exploded Mrs. Hastings, glaring at him. "Homely, indeed! Tom is the best-looking boy in Hastings. If I am putting this picture away, it's because it doesn't do him justice."

Tom came clattering up the steps at that very minute. Then what do you suppose Mrs. Hastings did? She darted out into the hall, and she gave Tom a great big hug, and she never even noticed that he was hot and dirty.

Tom was astonished, absolutely astonished, so astonished that he confided to Charlie later in the day, "You know, Charlie, I've found out something. Women are funny—even my mother!"

Black Magic

Weeks went by, and summer slipped into autumn with a change so gradual as to pass almost unnoticed. It was not the flaming gold and red and purple autumn of other years, but a sober world of dull yellows and browns as a result of the hot, rainless summer. Yet the sumac blazed forth along the roadside, and goldenrod and purple asters added quiet spots of color to the fields of dead, brown grasses.

School began once more, but each Saturday afternoon found boys like Tom and Charlie racing away down country roads, eager to strip the hazel bushes or to shake the last few nuts from the hickory trees. At times they stopped in their mad dash to watch the wild geese passing high overhead or to fill their pockets with thorn apples from the thorn-apple trees along the roadside.

One Saturday afternoon there was no Jim Hastings among the groups of hurrying boys. Old Doctor Wheeler's horse had cut his foot on a stone. The doctor had some calls to make in a neighboring town. He was to borrow a horse and buggy from the Hastings' stable; and Jim, thrilled at the idea, was to ride along with him.

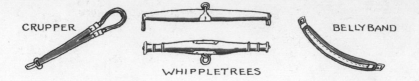

CRUPPER BELLY BAND

WHIPPLETREES

At the moment Flash, the chestnut-brown trotter, was cutting capers in the Hastings' stable. Jim had just taken down the harness from its peg on the wall and had thrown it over the horse's back.

"Whoa, Flash, whoa!" coaxed Jim, as the horse sidled around in the stall, trying his best to get out from under. "Behave yourself, can't you?"

But Flash had no idea of behaving himself.

"Like as not, he won't take the crupper," thought Jim the next minute. The crupper was a leather strap fastened to the harness. It went under the horse's tail to help keep the harness in place. Flash knew what was coming as well as Jim did. He had been harnessed many times before.

When Jim tried to lift the tail and put the crupper in place, Flash held his tail down tight. Jim coaxed and pulled until he was red in the face. Still he couldn't budge that tail.

"Just for this, you won't get any oats tonight," he panted, stopping to rest his arms.

"Give him a slap where it will do the most good," grinned the doctor, coming into the barn at that moment with his bag in his hand.

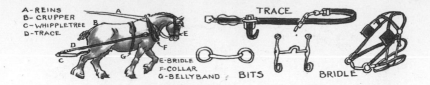

A-REINS
B-CRUPPER
C-WHIPPLETREE
D-TRACE
E-BRIDLE
F-COLLAR
G-BELLYBAND
TRACE
BITS
BRIDLE

Flash knew better than to fool with the doctor. So he let Jim lift his tail and put it through the strap, and the crupper was soon in place.

Jim buckled the bellyband and made everything fast. Then he backed the horse out of the stall onto the barn floor, ready to put on the bridle. When he tried to put the bit into the horse's mouth, Flash threw up his head and shut his teeth tight together. Jim was tall for his age, but he couldn't reach when Flash held his head high.

"Come on! Hold your head down, that's a good fellow," coaxed Jim.

The head came down, but Flash wouldn't take the bit. He had to have his fun first, and he was having a great time teasing Jim.

"Put your thumb into his mouth back of his teeth," suggested Doctor Wheeler. "That will do the business!"

When Jim did that, Flash opened his mouth far enough to let the bit slip between his teeth. When Jim pulled the horse's ears down to crowd them under the bridle strap, Flash almost seemed to wink at him. Maybe he didn't wink, but there was mischief in his eye; and Jim had to laugh in spite of himself.

"I'll lift up the thills while you back him in," said Doctor Wheeler.

Flash shook his head and slobbered all over Jim's hand, but he finally backed between the thills of the buggy. A minute later the tugs were fastened to the whippletrees, and the rest of the harnessing was completed. "Giddap," called the doctor, as Jim jumped onto the seat beside him. Flash trotted quickly away up the River Road.

It was a lovely autumn day, warm as summer. When the buggy passed "diving rock" in the river north of Hastings, Jim heard a voice shouting,

"The last one in is a monkey's uncle!"

Immediately a group of boys on the bank dropped their clothes where they stood, and Tom and Sam and Charlie dived into the water.

"Don't swallow the whole river! I need it to swim in!" shouted Jim, as Flash trotted past.

"Too bad—missing the fun, Jim," said the doctor. "But never you mind, lad! You'll have something better to talk about tonight than swimming and nut gathering."

"I will? What?" asked Jim, wide-eyed and eager.

"Magic, black magic," teased the doctor.

"What is it? Where is it?" demanded Jim.

"Oh, it's just a queer machine in Mr. Browning's store in Oak Grove, where we are going," drawled the doctor. "You put a contraption to your ear, and upon my word, lad, the voice of someone talking a mile away comes out of that thing as plain as day."

"Aw! Who says so?" retorted Jim.

"I do! I saw it with my own eyes and heard it with my own ears," insisted Doctor Wheeler. "There's another contraption you talk into; and believe it or not, you don't even have to shout. Your voice travels along a wire—a wire, mind you—and someone a mile away can hear you."

All the rest of the way to Oak Grove, Jim sat tilted on the edge of the seat. One question wasn't answered before another was on the way. The only trouble was that Doctor Wheeler didn't know very much, not half enough to satisfy Jim.

"Land sakes, lad, you've got me all tuckered out!" declared the doctor in desperation. "Tele—telephone! That's what you call it. It's only about three years old, and a man by the name of Bell had the idea. Now don't ask more questions because I can't answer them. That's all I know!" But it didn't occur to Jim to keep still.

Never were there longer minutes than those Jim spent, sitting outside one house and then another, waiting for the doctor. "Oh, botheration!" he kept repeating until even Flash felt the suspense and whinnied and pawed the dust in excitement. Even when the doctor was through at last, Flash had to be watered and firmly tethered to the hitching rail about the town square, with his nose bag under his chin. Only then could Jim and the doctor make a beeline for Mr. Browning's store.

Sure enough, there on the wall was the telephone, and crowded round it was a group of very curious people. The telephone consisted of two brown wooden boxes joined together by wires. On one of the boxes were two small, flat bells; and hanging from a hook underneath, was the "contraption" which Doctor Wheeler said you put to your ear. On the other box was another contraption something like a small horn, into which you talked.

All the time Mr. Browning was doing up bundles, he was waiting for the bell to ring. But the bell didn't ring. Nothing happened! Not one thing! Everyone grew fidgety and more fidgety.

When at last the bell did ring, everyone jumped, even Mr. Browning. He dropped the bundle he was wrapping. Then he walked over to the wall with a broad smile on his face.

"Who wants to try? Who wants to hear a voice from far away?" he asked.

No one stirred. That telephone was so new and strange that not a single person would make a move in its direction.

"Why, gentlemen!" exclaimed Mr. Browning, with a smile which grew broader and broader.

"It's so simple a child can operate it. Come on, son, show them how it is done."

Before Jim knew what had happened, he was standing in front of the boxes with one contraption to his ear. The next thing he knew, he was saying a very shaky hello into the other contraption, which looked a little like a horn.

Instantly a look of astonishment came over his face. "Someone is talking!" he exclaimed. "I can hear him just as plain. He is saying hello and asking me what I want today."

"Go ahead and answer," urged Mr. Browning.

But how could Jim answer? He didn't know what he wanted. He squirmed around on one foot and then the other.

"Go ahead! Say something! It won't bite! There is nothing to be afraid of," urged Mr. Browning.

Jim braced up. Everyone was laughing at him. He had to say something! He had to say something to someone a mile away! So he shouted, "How's the weather down there?"

Why he asked about the weather, Jim never knew; but from far away came a voice which said, "Just what it is back your way! If it doesn't rain, we'll have a long dry spell." That's what the voice said, and only Jim could hear it.

Jim walked out of that store in a daze. Was it he or some other boy to whom this wonderful thing had happened? Had he really talked over a telephone, or was he only dreaming? But by the time he reached the buggy, he was back to earth again. Land, what a story he'd have to tell the boys! Land, how glad he was that Flash had had a rest and a nose bag of oats to speed him on his way!

"Don't you think I could drive a while?" he asked the doctor. "I feel just like driving."

"Why not?" said Doctor Wheeler, handing over the reins and reaching for his pipe.

Flash trotted along at a lively pace. He knew the road and was glad to be on the homeward trail. Driving meant little more to Jim than holding the reins. So he had time aplenty to think; and with every clop of the horse's feet, his story got bigger and bigger.

But not even Jim realized how big a story it would turn out to be. When the *Hastings Herald* came out that week, there on the front page was a picture of Jim. "First Boy to Talk over Telephone." That's what the headlines said. No wonder Jim was grinning from ear to ear! Not many boys can create a sensation like that! Not many!

Spring Thaw

November days passed quickly by. Dry leaves swirled from the trees, and the bare branches shook in the whistling wind. Purple-cold clouds hurried across the sky; and Hastings, lonely and wind-swept, seemed waiting for the long winter.

For years to come, this was to be remembered as "The Winter of the Big Snows." November was scarcely over before the first snow began, sweeping softly, steadily, endlessly out of the northwest. When the storm ended, there came a few days of dazzling brightness when the sun rose on a hushed white world and set in a flame of color across the sky. Then swirling out of the north came another storm of heavier snow. So the winter continued.

"You know the rain we missed last summer," remarked Mr. Lake after the first storm. "Well, here it is! A little late, I admit, but worth a fortune for our fields and gardens!"

So thought everyone in Hastings. But as one storm followed closely upon another, men were not so pleased and not so confident. The dangers of a sudden spring thaw led to anxious headshakes.

These were the days when smart-looking
cutters skimmed across the snow, making paths of
their own above the fence tops. The mule car and
the yellow wagon of the fat little butcher slipped
along on runners; and Thunder and Lightning, the
old brown mules, made music of their own with
the jingle of their bells. Boys hitched their sleds

to every passing cutter and rode gaily about town and far out into the country, only to trudge home for miles through the snow and cold.

Day after day and week after week, wintry winds found their way into the cracks and crannies of every house in Hastings. Frost covered even the keyholes and lay so thick on the windows that a twilight darkness filled the rooms at midday. Only the fire shining red through the isinglass doors of the base-burners shed a cheerful glow. Only the base-burners, and the red-hot cookstoves in kitchens where teakettles sang from morning till night, ready at a moment's notice to thaw out the frozen pumps by the kitchen doors!

Coal buckets were forever empty, wood boxes forever waiting to be filled, and each trip to the woodshed was longer and colder than the one before. Trudging through the snow to care for the cattle and the horses was hateful work, while chapped hands and frostbitten ears and noses made everyone miserable. There was something more to winter in Hastings than just gay cutter rides across the snow.

Then one February morning Hastings awoke to the drip, drip, dripping sound of melting icicles on the roofs.

"The thaw has begun," said anxious voices, as the snowbanks began to sink away. All day streams of water in swirls and eddies raced down the hills to the Big Turtle.

"A few days of this and we're in for trouble," said Silas Lane soberly, as he stood in the door of his woolen mill, with eyes fixed upon the water racing along above the ice-covered river.

No sooner were the people of Hastings in bed that night than great slashes of rain beat against the windowpanes, rain which continued all night and through the next two days.

At noon of the second day Doctor Wheeler was home at last from a country call over almost impassable roads where his buggy sank hub-deep in slush and mud. Home with alarming news! The ice was going out up the river.

Before many hours the ice could be seen coming, enormous cakes, carried along by the furious rush of the water. The ice managed somehow to slip under the first bridges, only to jam the tighter against the Fox Street bridges and the railroad bridge to the south.

Hundreds of people lined both shores of the river and watched the ice jam sway the long railroad bridge back and forth. Even as they watched, a train suddenly appeared upon the bridge. Men and women stood motionless, waiting in breathless suspense for what was to happen next. Boys like Tom and Charlie began to shout, "It's Big Bill and the *Prairie Flyer*, and the bridge is going down!" Then instantly their shouts died in their throats, and they, too, stood motionless.

Luck was with Big Bill that day—fool's luck, Old Joe called it. Under full steam the engine took the bridge! Under full steam it reached the opposite bank! A shout of relief and admiration burst from the watching crowd. Yet only an hour later the railroad bridge went down.

In the middle of the night the covered bridges at Main and Fox streets were swept away with a crashing roar. The long bridge across the river at New York Street still held, but now there was no way to reach the island except by boat.

Now the ice jam, having cleared a path before it, began to break up and rush away downstream. The danger was over, but the damage was left behind. Basements of mills and factories and stores were knee-deep in water, and goods stored in them were water-soaked and useless.

In the days which followed, tall tales were told in Hastings. Flour from Mr. Gray's mill was found on cakes of ice forty miles down the river. Stories were told of turtles hurrying from the river and climbing trees for safety. Ice cakes were found weeks later, lodged in the highest branches of the willows on Round Island.

Boats traveled back and forth from the island to both banks of the river. Though Tom and Charlie thought boat rides to the grocery store were a great lark, Mr. Steel and men like him on the island grew sober-faced and thoughtful, as their business fell off with every passing day.

Again Hastings was faced with a weighty problem. Bridges there must be, not wooden affairs for the next flood to wash away, but iron bridges to last forever. Where in the world was the money to come from?

One morning Mayor Hastings and Mr. Lane left on the *Prairie Flyer* for the State Capitol to talk to the governor. They returned with cheering news. Not only would the State grant permission to build the bridges, but if the town could raise the rest of the money, the State would help with a grant of four thousand dollars. This was almost one-third of the money needed to build two up-to-date iron bridges at Fox Street.

The great good news put heart and hope into everyone. Now Hastings *had* to do something! No town could afford to forfeit the money which the State stood ready to give. Once more the people were faced with an election to raise the property tax. But this time the increase was so small that even Dan Cutter used his reason.

"I'll be beat if I ever saw the likes of this town for running into trouble," he complained to Mayor Hastings on election morning.

"I'll be beat if you ever saw a town with as much spunk for pulling itself out by the bootstraps! If we get into trouble, we don't stay there! Come, admit it!" retorted the mayor.

His quick retort made Old Dan chuckle. "You're right, Tom," he grinned. "For once in your life, you're right. Your election will cost me twenty-five cents a year until the day I die, but even I can see that a bridge is worth it."

Summer's End

Spring came early to Hastings that year, a generous, joyous spring of showers and sunshine. There was life in the crisp spring air, an urge to be up and doing in the smell of growing grasses. And well for Hastings that it was that way! Gas mains and water mains to be laid! Bridges to be built, and a hundred other things in the space of one short summer!

No sooner was the frost out of the ground than the work began. Digging here, digging there, digging all over town! Weeks slipped quickly by, and north on the outskirts of town the big well was drilled deep down through underground rock. Across the road, on the knoll, the standpipe was rising high in the air. South along the west bank of the Big Turtle the brick buildings of the Gas Works rose one after another, and among the willows on Round Island stood the gasholder.

Spring merged into sultry summer, and still the work went on, gathering speed with each passing day. Interest created interest, and one idea gave rise to another until wholly unexpected things began to happen in Hastings.

Up in front of his new house on Elm Street, Joseph White was laying a walk, a brick walk, made from Hastings' own Cherry Red brick.

"Upon my word! Has it come to the point where even a good plank walk can't satisfy us?" chuckled John Gray, out for a stroll in his shirt sleeves, as he stopped to talk to the mayor and Joseph White, who were busily examining the new walk. "What's this town coming to?"

Anyone walking down a certain side street on the island would have come upon another surprising idea. Pavement was being laid, pavement of good, solid cedar blocks.

"We'll try it out here," decided the Town Council. "Then we'll know what to do another year. Once Broadway and River Street have had time to settle after all this digging, we'll use the money which the gas company paid the town, to put in pavement. It's time the business streets were pulled out of the dust and mud."

No doubt Big Jack Casey, the policeman, still had his troubles. But at any rate, there were no cows roaming the streets these days to annoy him. How could they roam without danger of breaking their legs?

"Come, Buttercup," grinned Old Joe one morning, as he tied Buttercup with a long rope to a tree in a nearby field. "Forget that you ever knew how to open a garden gate because you'll never open another. The Town Council played a trick on you last night."

Old Joe was right. "Now that we've got the cows off the streets, we'll see to it that they stay off," declared the Town Council when they passed this "blue law." Five dollars fine for any cow, horse, goat, mule, or donkey allowed to run at large on the streets of Hastings!

Not many days later Old Joe was busy with his hammer, knocking down the high board fence around his front yard.

"Is your woodpile running low?" demanded Big Bill on his way home to Pigeon Hill.

"It's as high as it ever was," insisted Old Joe. "But what's the use of a fence when the cows are locked up? You wouldn't have me keep it for its beauty, now would you?"

"Not I!" laughed Big Bill, stopping to give Old Joe a lift with the boards. "In fact, I might even follow your example."

Still the weeks slipped by; and by mid-August, Tom was singing in the bathtub at the end of the upstairs hall. Why he sang he never knew, but sing he did every time he stepped into the big tin tub with the Cherry Red woodwork all around.

Never before had there been so many things to keep boys alert, excited, and interested. When the heavy iron framework for the bridges was swung into place, Tom and Charlie had to be fairly dragged home long enough to eat their dinners. When the time came to place the lampposts along Broadway, River Street, and Island Avenue, the boys superintended the placing of every post.

Finally came the night when the lights were to be turned on for the first time. Every road leading into town brought its crowd of hurrying people. Down on Broadway, on River Street, and on the Island, excitement was running high. Crowds lined the sidewalks and overflowed into the streets, waiting for the great moment to arrive.

Then out from the Town Hall came the mayor, a lighted taper in one hand, a small ladder under his arm. Behind him came all the men of the gas company who had helped to make this great moment possible. One at a time they mounted the ladder. One at a time the lamps were lighted until Hastings was ablaze with light.

Down the streets moved the lamplighters while
the crowds cheered and surged about them. If
certain men like Banker Hastings, Silas Lane, Mr.
James Hastings, and Mr. Samuel White stepped
aside to let boys like Tom and Jim and Sam and
Charlie take their places, surely they were not

afraid to mount a ladder and light a gas lamp. Surely they had a better reason.

Back and forth through the lighted streets surged the crowds until long after bedtime. Finally Banker Hastings, with Tom beside him, turned the noses of his high-stepping grays up the long Main Street hill and drew to a stop in front of "The House on the Hill." There at the gate in the white picket fence stood Grandfather and Grandmother, gazing quietly down at the lighted streets of Hastings.

"All this," murmured Grandfather softly, "all this in one short year and a little more."

Some time later Tom lay wide-eyed and sleepless in his big black-walnut bed. His mother slipped softly in to try the gas jet; but Tom, busy with his own thoughts, did not say a word. "All this in one short year and a little more." What would Hastings be like when he was a man? Tom wished he knew.

CITY on the HILL
1910

Weary Waiting

Tom Hastings, nicknamed Pinkie, was fidgety, very fidgety, indeed. He couldn't read. He couldn't sit still. He was as uneasy as a bad conscience. That's what his father remarked with a good-natured grin as the continual squeaking of Pinkie's tilt-back chair by the window caused Mr. Hastings to look up from his work at his huge roll-top desk.

RUBBER STAMPS PAPERWEIGHT PRESS LETTER FILE INKWELLS

Pinkie flushed red through his freckles and returned the grin over his left shoulder. Then came a sigh from his toes up, a sigh which proclaimed more plainly than words that he was doing the best he could. What more should you expect from a boy who has been waiting the livelong day for something important to happen and must still go on waiting?

For the sake of something better to do, Pinkie pulled his chair closer to the window and sat with his elbows on the broad window sill. Then, with his chin cupped in his hands, he stared down from the second-story window into the bustling hollow of the street below.

It was midsummer, and the city was the large and busy one to which Pinkie's father came every weekday morning from his home in Hastings forty miles away to his work in the General Offices of the Hastings, Lake Shore, and Western Railroad.

Delivery trucks and grocery carts and huge yellow ice wagons went clattering by, as the horses' shoes

struck out a dull clop, clop on the cobbles. Empty
farm wagons lumbered heavily along on their way
home from the markets on Water Street. "City
horses are gangly-looking nags," thought Pinkie,
"but good pullers. Country horses are big and
powerful, but clumsy, and what do they amount
to when it comes to speed?"

Even as Pinkie was thinking, the driver of the
sprinkling wagon, returning from his morning
round, spied a clear place in the everlasting procession of carts and wagons and sent a last burst
of water over the hot, dusty cobbles. The man
alighting from the streetcar at the corner darted
to safety, but the very fashionable woman in the
peg-top skirt and the Merry Widow hat hobbled
down the car steps directly into the spray.

Pinkie gasped and let out a low chuckle.
Instantly the angry clang, clang of the streetcar
gong screeched, "What do you think you are doing?
What do you think you are doing?" Then the

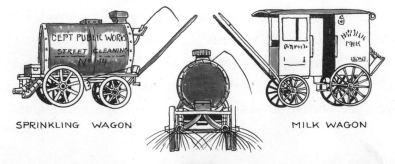

SPRINKLING WAGON   MILK WAGON

219

driver of the sprinkling wagon poked out his head to view half in alarm and half in amusement the trouble he had left behind him.

The Merry Widow hat disappeared from sight, and now Pinkie sat alert, his arms tense on the arms of the squeaking chair. Weaving in and out among the carts and wagons like a little black fly, came a Rambler. That's what it must be! One of the first cars ever made! Five or six years old if it were a day! Old-fashioned as could be! Why, look! A dashboard as on a buggy, and even a place for a whip! Great carriage wheels with wire spokes and hard rubber tires, and one seat facing backward! Only a lever to steer by! A one cylinder — that's what it was — a "one lunger"! That was the reason for all the noise!

Another minute and that "one lunger" was creating plenty of excitement. Horses were balking and snorting, drivers were pulling hard on the reins, while a mounted policeman, riding along by the side of the Rambler, was giving the owner a piece of his mind. What did he mean, bringing this "devil wagon" into a busy city street? Starting a few runaways — was that what he was figuring on doing? Turn to the right at the next corner, and be quick about it, too!

If only the policeman had kept his temper! If only the Rambler's owner hadn't become so confused that he pulled every lever he could lay his hands upon! With a spurt and a snort, the Rambler's engine died under the very noses of two chestnut-brown horses that shied in fright and almost lifted the big plume-covered hats from the heads of the two ladies who were sitting in the seat facing backward. Only the big veils which covered the plumes and which were tied under their chins saved the day. Of course they were wearing veils. No lady's face could stand the rush of wind in a horseless carriage going ten miles an hour.

Instantly an amusing thought darted through Pinkie's head. "They are like my mother," he grinned. "They've been adding a new plume to the same old hat for the last dozen years."

At that very minute the telephone on the wall behind Pinkie rang loudly. He sprang to his feet and stood for a moment, breathless, mouth open, all the pent-up anticipation of the day shining in his eyes. But before his father could push back his papers and walk around the desk corner to the big brown box on the wall, Pinkie was by his side, whispering excitedly, "It's ready! That's Mr. Samson calling! I know it is!"

"Settle down!" ordered Mr. Hastings, but his broad smile and the tone of his voice showed that he was as excited as Pinkie.

"Hello, Samson?" Mr. Hastings was saying the next minute. "Ready, you say? We'll be at your bicycle shop in ten minutes. No, don't drive it around. Market Street is too busy to risk doing that at this time of day. By the way, don't forget the patches! It's forty miles to Hastings, and the road is none too good."

"Well, Tom, my boy," grinned Mr. Hastings, when the telephone conversation was over, "here we go! Shall we get ready now or wait until we reach the bicycle shop?"

"Now!" burst forth Tom, as his father rolled down the top of his desk without even straightening up his papers and turned to open the closet door in one corner of the room. From the closet Mr. Hastings took two long linen coats called dusters, two caps with broad visors, and two pairs of big goggles. From the pocket of the man-sized duster hung a pair of workingman's gloves.

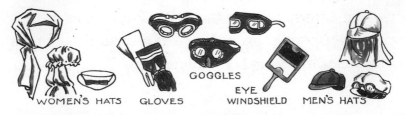

WOMEN'S HATS   GLOVES   GOGGLES   EYE WINDSHIELD   MEN'S HATS

The next minute Pinkie was a queer-looking sight, too queer-looking for Mr. Hastings, who declared with a chuckle, "I'll carry my own rigging until we reach the shop. I'd be the laughingstock of this place if I looked like you."

Now Mr. Hastings opened the door of the next office and stood for a moment in the doorway. It was a splendid office, furnished in the latest fashion, in shiny quartersawed oak.

"I'm off, Mr. President," he called laughingly to the old, white-haired, very dignified man at the roll-top desk.

Mr. Gates rose from his chair and joined the two adventurers in the doorway. The minute he saw Pinkie, his face was one complete smile.

"I hear you've acquired a nickname," he chuckled, "but how can I tell that you are Pinkie behind these things?" He took off Tom's goggles and tried them on himself. Then, with a twinkle in his eye, he turned to Mr. Hastings.

"To think that I should live to see the day when the chief engineer of the Hastings, Lake Shore, and Western Railroad went home to Hastings in a 'devil wagon'!" he chuckled. "Too bad your grandfather isn't alive to see you! He was a great hand for newfangled contraptions, your grand-

father. Well, see that you keep to the road which skirts the railroad right of way, and I'll have an engine ready to send to the rescue when you break down, as you're sure to do."

"We aren't going to break down," grinned Mr. Hastings, as he and Tom started down the hall. "But I admit I'd feel better if it were a good railroad engine."

Everyone they met on their way to the door had some good-natured remark for Mr. Hastings.

"Good-by, Old Man, if we never see you again!"

"Don't forget! You'll be sitting on a tank of gasoline all the way to Hastings!"

"Watch out for farmers! I've heard tell that they sprinkle nails in the road."

Pinkie wished to goodness that they would stop. When a man is chief engineer of a railroad, when he has to take care of all the washouts on the line and all the track trouble, he comes to believe that a railroad engine is the most wonderful thing in the world. That's just what Pinkie's father thought, and that was why it had taken Mother years to convince him that the Hastings family should have a motorcar. Every family of any importance in Hastings had had one long ago. Even Old Dan Cutter's son had a brand-new Model T Ford. But Pinkie's own family had gone right on riding in an old surrey and going to the next town by train, just because every one of them could ride on a pass and didn't have to pay his way.

"Anything to please!" his father had finally said after years of teasing. But now, if these men didn't stop their joking, he might change his mind. Even now he might, when the deal for the new automobile was almost completed.

At last they were in the street, and Pinkie noticed with a sideward glance that the Rambler had disappeared. If he had only known where Mr. Samson's bicycle shop was, nothing could have kept him from making for it on the run. But he didn't know, and so all he could do was to hurry his father along and keep up a continual chatter.

"Queer place to go for an automobile — to a bicycle shop," he began.

"Yes, it does seem queer on the face of it," replied Mr. Hastings. "But don't forget, Tom, bicycle mechanics have made some of the best automobiles we've had so far. The man who manufactured the car we are going to buy used to make bicycles and iceboxes and bird cages, too, so the story goes."

"Iceboxes! Bird cages! Are you sure it's a good car?" demanded Tom doubtfully.

"Wait until you see it!" answered Mr. Hastings. "It's a beauty, Tom! It went twenty miles an hour when I drove it for the first time yesterday."

Pierce Arrow

Finally they turned a corner, and Pinkie's watchful eye lighted upon a sign high overhead — JOE SAMSON, BICYCLE SHOP. Pinkie broke into a run which didn't stop until he stood speechless in front of a cherry-red touring car in the street in front of the shop.

Oh, what a car! A Pierce Arrow! Of course it was! Hadn't the Pierce Arrow made a fine showing in every reliability race it had ever entered? Might as well have a reliable car while you're about it! Away from the East — that's where it had come from! Swung high above the street, too, like a buggy to keep it out of the mud!

In the next half hour, while Pinkie's father talked and talked to Mr. Samson and pulled a lever here and turned a switch there and stepped on a pedal when there was nothing else to do, Pinkie examined that car from top to toe. Off came the goggles so that he could see better.

Enormous tires — pneumatic, filled with air like bicycle tires, only twenty times as big! A top which folded back over the rear seat just like a buggy top! Toolbox on the running board where it would be handy! Wing things over the wheels — fenders, that's what you called them! Headlights, taillight, and two big carriage lamps near the front seat! All the decorations of polished brass!

That tank on the running board — Pinkie knew what was in that! Acetylene gas! That's what it was! Special gas just for the lights! You turned on the gas with a key like the key you used to wind a clock. Then the gas began to flow through

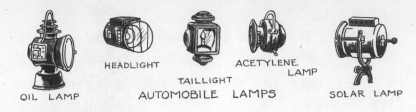

OIL LAMP   HEADLIGHT   ACETYLENE LAMP   SOLAR LAMP

TAILLIGHT

AUTOMOBILE LAMPS

the pipeline, and all you had to do was to open the glass door of each light and light the gas burner inside with a match.

When there was no more gas in the tank, you stopped at a bicycle shop, dropped off the old tank, and got a new one. Only be sure to keep the key! Three dollars a tank, that's about what you had to pay, so Mr. Samson said. Mighty expensive, that gas!

Now Mr. Samson and Father were going into the shop to talk business. Pinkie, with the warning not to touch a thing ringing in his ears, climbed into the front seat. No doors to the front seat! Just brace yourself and hold onto the seat arm if you didn't want to jolt out. Padded red leather seats to go with the color of the car! Look, the cushion of the driver's seat was pushed aside, and there underneath was the gas tank with the ruler on top, all ready to measure the gas.

Now Pinkie in all his glory was perched behind the wheel, pretending to steer. In front of him were the pedals and switches and levers which he was not supposed to touch. That big hand lever on the running board! That was the hand brake put there to help out the foot brake when the car had to stop on a hill. Better keep his hands off that! But the big rubber bulb which made the horn blow! That was another matter. Pinkie's fingers had been itching to squeeze that bulb for an hour past. Only a suspicion of what might happen if he did had kept him from trying. Now here it was, sticking enticingly up at his side. One squeeze could do no harm. Slow and easy now! Suddenly a harsh honk, honk exploded from the horn. The horse ahead reared on its hind legs, and Pinkie's suspicions came true.

"Tom Hastings, get out of that car this minute! What are you thinking of? Get into this shop and be quick about it!"

From that time on until business was over, Tom was on the inside of the shop looking out, squirming from one foot to the other and regretting that squeeze. He almost whooped with joy when his father at last put on his linen duster. Really,

AUTOMOBILE HORNS

if Mr. Hastings didn't look as ridiculous as Pinkie, he looked more so.

Another minute and Pinkie was back again in the front seat while Mr. Hastings, his linen duster sweeping the road, was busy with the crank.

"Did you say that some man had just invented a self-starter for an automobile?" he asked, after a few hard turns. "If so, I want one!"

"That's the story I've heard," replied Mr. Samson. "Watch out now, I warn you! That crank may fly back and break your arm. I've seen that happen many a time."

But the crank didn't. Half a dozen turns, which took all Mr. Hastings' strength and made his face very, very red, and the engine gave a welcome roar. Mr. Hastings made for the running board, jumped in beneath the wheel, and looked at Mr. Samson through his goggles.

"We're off!" he shouted, as excited as Tom by his side, and he reached for the handle of the gearshift.

"It's a grand car," beamed Mr. Samson, shaking his head to prove his words, "and you won't have any trouble if you don't start tinkering. Let those tinker who know how. By the way, here are some extra patches."

Get Out and Get Under

Forward over the cobbles went the splendid Pierce Arrow while people stood on the sidewalks to stare in admiration. Ten miles an hour! That's what the speedometer said! Not many cars had speedometers. You had to buy them extra. Good things to have, though! Kept you from going faster than the law allowed — ten miles an hour!

At once Mr. Hastings turned into a quieter side street and headed west toward the edge of the city. Oh, this was glorious! Even the smell of the gasoline!

"We're all right, Tom, as long as we're on the cobbles," he grinned, "but wait until we hit the dirt roads."

Maybe he was right, but, nevertheless, that car was shaking Tom from head to toe at that very minute. Still Tom didn't mind. They were good shakes. He enjoyed them, every one.

The minute the cobbles were left behind, Tom knew what his father was talking about. Dirt roads! Why call them that? Stone roads, that's what they were. Stones, dozens of them, flew to

AUTOMOBILE SPEEDOMETERS

right and left and banged against the brand-new fenders. Not stones — rocks. Pinkie jounced up and down, up and down. He couldn't stick to that slippery leather seat no matter how hard he tried. While his father, slowing down his speed, was going from one side of the road to the other, sighting the level places, the Pierce Arrow let out one rattle and then another. Every nut in the whole car would be shaken loose by the time they reached Hastings, every single nut!

"Thank goodness, it hasn't rained for weeks. At least, we won't get stuck in the mud," said Mr. Hastings with a sigh of relief, as they came to a stretch of dirt road that was really dirt road, shaded by big, overhanging maples.

Now the car gained speed, and Mr. Hastings, mind free, could carry on a conversation and drive at the same time.

"You know, Tom," he began thoughtfully, "this road isn't a bit better than it was almost seventy years ago when your grandfather came over it in a stagecoach when he was a boy. A little wider, perhaps, but worn down until it is even more rocky."

"Was this the Old Coach Road Grandfather came over with Lightning Joe?" asked Pinkie, catching his breath in surprise and wonder.

"The very road!" answered his father. "Five
hours from now it will bring us straight to Hastings." After a moment he added, "But stagecoach
days are over; and if we are to have motorcars, it's
time we did something about roads like this."

Now the maples were left behind, and the road
stretched straight ahead through the treeless
prairies. Farm lands rolled easily away to the
horizon, and golden fields of headed grain were
interspersed with the green of waving corn. Overhead was the great gray-blue, heat-laden sky of
midsummer. The sun shone hot on the fields, hot

on the widening stretches of road that came
forward to meet them. Dust rolled up in clouds
behind them, cut into their faces with the hot
wind of the moving car, and settled thick and
gray on the cherry-red paint and on the seat beside
them.

A few more miles and the road grew rutty with
wagon tracks. Again they jounced and bounced
along. A work horse, grazing at ease in a field
near the roadside, snorted and dashed to safety
at the other end of the field. Now and then they
passed a farm wagon or two, or an occasional
farmer in his buggy. Horses balked and shied
or simply shivered their fright as the car bumped
past. Once an angry farmer cut at them with his
buggy whip.

Suddenly they came upon another car — a new Maxwell — stalled by the side of the road.

"Lend me some gas?" asked the driver, as Mr. Hastings pulled up beside him. "I should have bought some at the grocery store in the last town, but I've had four punctures in the last hour! Too upset to remember gas!"

Mr. Hastings reached into the back of the car and handed him one of the five-gallon cans which Mr. Samson had put there for an emergency.

"Think nothing of it," he said, as the man offered to pay. "Five gallons of gas at nine cents a gallon won't hurt anyone."

"Suppose we leave it this way," said the stranger. "I live five miles up the road in a white house with a big stone barn. Drive in someday when you are passing and help yourself from the tank in the barn. The Standard Oil wagon stops twice a week, and the tank is never empty."

"I will if I need to," called back Mr. Hastings, as the Pierce Arrow again started on its way.

Soon the road turned, and for a long time it skirted the railroad right of way. Pinkie waved exultantly to a train crew that went flying by.

"Do you think anyone will ever make an auto that can go as fast as an engine?" he asked.

"I wouldn't be surprised," smiled Mr. Hastings. "See that stretch of track, Tom? Something important is going to happen there soon. You see, when I was a boy, Mr. Gates told me I couldn't make an engine that could go seventy-five miles an hour; or, if I did, I couldn't make track that would stand the strain. I helped make both the track and the engine long ago, and now what? He says we need an engine that can go ninety, and what am I going to do about it?"

"What are you going to do? What are you?" demanded Tom eagerly.

"Going to try out an engine on that stretch of track! An engine and three or four new steel cars so that the engine won't run too light!"

"Will it do ninety? Can it?" Tom broke in.

"Don't spread the good news," chuckled Mr. Hastings. "I'm counting on its doing more."

Suddenly Pinkie gave a bounce that was not caused by any stone in the road.

"Suppose when I'm a man, I make an automobile that can go faster than your engine?" he said.

"That's an idea," declared his father. "Suppose you do; and while you're about it, make something besides paper-thin tires for it to run on. Remember, I had to make the track."

Time went by, and father and son grew used to riding. Were there bumps in the road? None to speak of! Did they mind the heat and the dust? Why should they, in the cool breeze of a moving car? All they could feel — more and more and more and more — was the thrill of riding in an automobile. It was the grandest sport in the world.

"We'll make it, Tom, in five hours, just as I said we would, without a speck of trouble," boasted Mr. Hastings, as they passed the big Driving Park outside of town where the horse races were held every spring and fall. Ahead of them, two miles away, smoke soared from the factory chimneys of Hastings. Home in another half hour, with Mother and Peggy watching and waiting! Home, driving the finest car in town!

Now the Driving Park was behind them. Mr. Derby's farm, Mr. Carpenter's, and Mr. Barber's yet to go! Then pavement, the good brick pavement of Main Street!

Suddenly a pop, a whistle of escaping air, a wobbling front wheel, a foot on the brake pedal, and stop!

"A puncture almost within hailing distance of home!" exploded Mr. Hastings in disgust, as he pulled the jack from the toolbox.

One nut which held the rim in place was unscrewed, then the next, and the next, and the next. With a great pull, off came the tire rim. Something in the air made Pinkie sense that it was no time to say a word. He stood quietly by his father's side as the tire was pulled from the rim with a rubbery flop. He didn't even offer to help.

Mr. Hastings stopped long enough to wipe the sweat from his eyes with the sleeve of his linen duster. Then he set to work to examine the tire and pull the tube from the casing. He hoped that he wouldn't need water to find the hole. He didn't! There it was! A tack, its head buried in the thin

TIRE TESTING TIRE TOOLS TIRES GAS TANK GASOLINE MEASURES GENERATOR

rubber of the tire! A dark suspicion crossed his mind.

"Look in the road ahead there. See if you can find any more of these," he said to Tom. Tom looked and found — not one, but half a dozen tacks directly ahead of the car.

"So that's what you're up to, Farmer Derby," thought Mr. Hastings, as he pulled the tube from the casing, found the hole, smeared on cement, and set the patch in place.

While the patch was drying, Pinkie and his father sat on a stone beside the road. Mr. Hastings said that they should thank their lucky stars that it was suppertime. No one from Hastings would come along at this hour. He would hate to have anyone find him in this predicament with a brand-new car. No sooner were the words out of his mouth than over the hill from Hastings came young Doctor Wheeler in his father's buggy.

"Time to put in a good word for Old Dobbin," he grinned, as he drew up beside them.

Tom was as mad as a hatter, but Mr. Hastings just looked amused and a bit sheepish.

Another moment, however, and Doctor Wheeler forgot to poke fun in admiration for the car.

"It's a beauty, all right! How does it seem to be the owner of a car like that? Too bad to have a puncture the very first thing! But then, you must get used to that! Probably will have half a dozen every time you go for a ride!"

By the time Doctor Wheeler was through looking the car over, the patch was dry. He helped Mr. Hastings put the tube back into the casing and ease the tire back onto the rim. He even took his turn at the hand pump until the tire was hard once more.

"Don't tell about the puncture," warned Pinkie, as the Doctor climbed back into his buggy.

"I'll do my best to remember," grinned Doctor Wheeler. "But you'd better remind me, Pinkie, every day or two."

One hour it had taken to change that tire! One full hour! It was a hot, tired, sticky, and very

DETAIL OF INTERIOR
AUTOMOBILE PUMPS

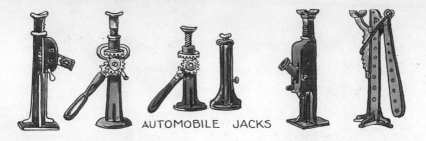

AUTOMOBILE JACKS

dirty Mr. Hastings who cranked the car once more. But not five minutes after Tom and he were in the front seat, the annoyance of the last hour was all forgotten. Already they could hear the admiring ohs and ahs of Mother and Peggy. Already they could see the delight and surprise in their eyes.

Now the Old Coach Road led through the outskirts of Hastings, where the homes of the ever-growing city were pushing out and out with each passing year. Big square houses on every side, new-fashioned, without a single tower or cupola to spoil their simplicity!

On rolled the Pierce Arrow over pavement of the good Cherry Red brick for which Hastings was famous. Elm trees and maples arched high overhead. Behind the hedges on either side, old-fashioned houses, grown too ornate for good looks and too big for modern housewives to take care of, stood in lonely-looking grandeur.

Ahead of the car a long hill sloped gently down into the valley of the Big Turtle River, and all up and down the hill was the ceaseless movement of traffic, the noise and bustling activity of a big city.

Facing the Old Coach Road on the hilltop, with the smoke and the office buildings of the city reaching up to encircle it, stood "The House on the Hill." Pinkie's great-grandfather had built that rambling, green-shuttered, friendly-looking white house. His grandfather had lived there, and now his father and Pinkie himself. Someone by the name of Hastings had always lived there since that long-ago day when the beams and uprights and clapboards for its building had been cut from trees in the Big Woods. But now the city, which had had its beginnings in that house-raising, was reaching up to claim "The House on the Hill." Already Pinkie's father and mother were talking of a newer and quieter home in the suburbs.

The Pierce Arrow turned in at the drive which circled the stone wall round the old-fashioned well. Ohs and ahs from Mother and squeals of delight from Peggy greeted Father and Tom as the Pierce Arrow stopped before the front door.

With never a thought for the dust, Mother and Peggy climbed into the back seat. Once, twice, half a dozen times the car circled the long carriage drive under the two big maples while Peggy repeated in one continual stream, "Isn't it grand, Tom! Isn't it!"

"Look here, Peggy, look here!" called Tom, as he pointed out one marvel and then another.

Little by little, the sparkle of excitement in Mother's eyes changed to a softer, quieter look of complete pleasure and satisfaction, and Father smiled a proud smile at her every time he turned a corner.

Finally the drive was circled for the last time. Father turned the nose of the car into the carriage house where Old Martin, the stableman and gardener, his face beaming with admiration, had moved the fringe-topped surrey to the far corner. No sooner had the Hastings family alighted from the car than Father, Tom, and Old Martin set to work with a will, wiping off dust and polishing brass. Not until dark could the repeated calls of Mother, Peggy, and Ellen, the cook, bring them into the house to a belated supper.

In the meantime, in the big white barn, two well-matched, high-stepping grays munched their oats contentedly and went to sleep in their stalls, with never an inkling of the fact that, for them, "the days of the horse were over."

Spreading the News

No sooner had Pinkie opened his eyes the next morning than a dozen pleasant thoughts surged through his head. "Grandmother's for breakfast!" he decided before his bare feet touched the coolness of the polished floor. Not three minutes later he bounded down the back stairs and bumped into Ellen as he raced for the kitchen door.

"Excuse me! I'm sorry!" he called, as the screen door closed behind him and a plate of hot biscuits went sailing across the floor.

Out in the carriage house Old Martin was whistling "In the Shade of the Old Apple Tree" and polishing brass which didn't need polishing.

"If Charlie Lane gets here before I get back, don't let him touch that car!" cautioned Pinkie. He stopped long enough to beam all over at the sight of the Pierce Arrow and to give the horn one squeeze. The next minute he was poking his nose against the screen of the dining-room window. Inside he could see the back of his mother's head with its Psyche knot of dark brown hair.

"I'm not hungry! I couldn't eat a bite!" he pleaded. "I'm going to Grandmother's. She's expecting me."

"Run along, whirlwind! We'll eat in comfort
without you," called his father's voice. "Tell
Grandmother and Grandfather that we'll be around
this evening to give them a ride."

Up Main Street sailed Tom. He ran until he
couldn't catch another breath. Then he sighted
a big yellow ice wagon, hopped up on the back
step, and helped himself to a handful of chips.
The iceman had been at work since five in the
morning. He had already cut many five-hundred-
pound pieces into fifties and twenty-fives. So
there were plenty of chips.

Just as Pinkie let go of a big piece of ice which was freezing his fingers and making them feel red-hot at the same time, he spied two acquaintances of his walking along together. One was William, the scissors-grinder, wheeling his grindstone to the ding-dong accompaniment of a bell. No one ever called him Bill or Will, just William. Grandmother said that was because he had seen better days. William was sober-faced. He seldom smiled, but he did good work.

With him was Tony, the umbrella mender, little and dark, lighthearted and gay. He had a bell, also, but he wasn't ringing it yet. William and Tony always walked along together and smoked a morning pipe of tobacco. Then they separated, and one took one part of the city and one the other. No housewife had money enough to have her scissors sharpened and her umbrella mended on the same day.

"Hello, William! Hello, Tony!" called Pinkie. "You ought to see our new automobile!"

"How many times must I tell you to keep off this ice wagon?" growled the driver, discovering Pinkie for the first time.

By this time the ice wagon had reached the corner of Maple Avenue. That was as far as Pinkie wanted to go, anyway. So off he hopped.

The trolley car was coming down Maple Avenue on its return trip from the end of the line. Pinkie wished that he had been on it to see the sparks sputter from the electric wires overhead as the motorman turned the trolley. It was an open, summertime car with seats running crosswise. On either side was a long step along which the conductor walked when he collected the fares. Hundreds of people went for a trolley ride every evening. It was a splendid way to cool off.

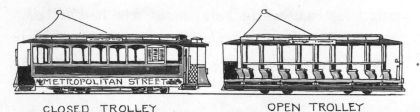

CLOSED TROLLEY   OPEN TROLLEY

The car passed, and Pinkie whistled as he walked along in the green sunlight under the maples. In the street beside him easygoing milk horses stamped the pavement and seemed to stop more often than they started. Men on their way to work passed by with pleasant "good mornings."

One swing on the ring in the horse's head on the hitching post, and Pinkie bounded up the long brick walk to Grandmother's house.

If there was an extra place at the breakfast table, that was nothing unusual. There was always an extra place, and Pinkie was generally on hand to fill it. For a boy who couldn't eat a bite, it was surprising the amount of oatmeal and milk which disappeared within the next few minutes. Between bites Pinkie was extolling the merits of the Pierce Arrow, and Grandmother and Grandfather, opening their eyes wider and wider, said that such things couldn't be true.

Outside of his own mother and father, Pinkie was sure that there were no two people in the world like Grandfather and Grandmother.

Grandmother had big bright eyes that sparkled and then looked soft very quickly. She didn't like to be told things. She liked to think about them until she found them out for herself. Then she would tell Pinkie what she had found out. Her white hair waved softly and didn't stick out with "rats" and puffs underneath the way other women's hair did. Yet she did wear a net collar with ruching round the top, which came away up under her ears and was held in place by little pieces of whalebone.

Grandfather was a very old man — seventy-two this coming winter. He had soft white hair, also, and a goatee which made him look very distinguished. He had come to Hastings in a big brown stagecoach when he was a boy; and when he grew up, he had been president of the Hastings Bank. Only now he wasn't! He had had sense enough to give way to a younger man while he could still enjoy life. But he continued to go down to the bank every morning, and the Hastings National Bank was still the best bank in the city. Perhaps that was because Grandfather kept his eye on it.

When Pinkie explained about the evening ride, Grandfather was afraid Grandmother couldn't go. She would be sure to think that she was still riding in a buggy and would cry "Whoa!" and expect the car to stop every time she came to a hill. If Grandfather thought it was clever to say that, Grandmother soon turned the tables with a clever trick of her own.

Of course, Grandfather was going to stop in to
see the car on his way to the bank. Nothing could
stop him! When Tom and he stepped into the
surrey, Grandmother stepped right up behind them.
If anyone was going to see the new car, she was,
too. So Grandfather just said, "I declare! What's

the world coming to, anyway?" Then away they went down the street together.

The minute his eye lighted upon Old Martin, Pinkie demanded, "Has Charlie been here yet? What did he say?"

"He's green with envy!" declared Old Martin, not because Charlie *was* green with envy but because Old Martin knew that that was what Pinkie wanted him to say. Pinkie grinned from ear to ear. That was exactly the way Charlie ought to feel.

It was fortunate that Grandfather didn't have to be at the bank at any particular time. When he was through admiring the car and Grandmother had gone into the house with Mother, it was very late, indeed. Even if a car is wonderful, a fellow can't spend the whole day just looking. Pinkie thought he might as well ride downtown with Grandfather.

Now, if someone had told Pinkie that on the way downtown Grandfather and he would happen upon something that, in the days to come, would be even more exciting than a Pierce Arrow, he would never have believed it — *never!* But that's the way life goes, and that's the unexpected way things happen.

Nickelodeon

No sooner had the surrey reached the big central fire barn at the foot of the hill than the fire gong rang. Grandfather drew up at the curb on the opposite side of the street. Through the open door of the fire station Pinkie could see the two big white fire horses, Captain and Old Hundred. He could see the harness, suspended in the air above them, drop down upon their backs as one of the firemen pulled a lever. The next minute the horses and the fire-engine crew were tearing up the hill, with every boy and girl on the downtown streets racing after. Tom had a good notion to go, too, until a chance remark of his grandfather's caused him to change his mind.

Just because Grandfather had had to stop the surrey, he noticed something. "Upon my word, Tom, work's begun on the old harness shop."

Now, it wasn't a harness shop Grandfather was talking about at all. It was a big two-story brick building that stood on Main Street not far from the river. Once there had been a harness shop there. Grandfather was always talking about the old harness maker and a shoemaker called Dan, who had kept shop there together when he was a

boy. But the brick building had replaced the
harness shop years ago.

However, Grandfather was partly right. Work
had begun, and carpenters with hammers and saws
and chisels were knocking out the whole first-floor
front of the building.

Grandfather slipped from the surrey to talk to
a portly, good-natured, bald-headed man on the
sidewalk; and Tom hopped out, too.

"So you've definitely decided to let Hastings go
to the dogs, Frank, in spite of all we can say,"
said Grandfather, with a serious, stern-looking face,

but with a twinkle in the eye, which was turned the other way.

"Come, now, Banker Hastings, you don't hold with folks who say that a moving-picture show will send people to the dogs, do you?" asked Mr. Frank Rhodes, in a tone of worried surprise.

"And if I do, will that stop you from opening up a nickelodeon in this building?" asked Grandfather, still stern and still twinkling.

"It will not!" declared Mr. Rhodes, though he looked very much disturbed. "There's no harm in a moving picture that makes people laugh. Come, now, is there? I'll tell you what I'll do. I'll give you a free pass to the first show I put on, and you can come and see for yourself."

"It won't be necessary!" chuckled Grandfather. "I'm planning on coming and bringing Tom here with me. You see, Frank, my father always cautioned me not to wake up in the morning with yesterday's ideas. If moving pictures are a new thing, I'm for them; and if the pictures need improving, let's improve them."

"I swan!" exploded Mr. Rhodes, who hadn't realized until then that Grandfather was joking.

Tom, meantime, could scarcely believe his ears. A nickelodeon, a moving-picture show in Hastings!

He had never seen a moving-picture show in all his life. Charlie Lane had seen one when he went to New York. "The Great Train Robbery!" That's what it was called! Horses getting bigger and bigger and riding right out of the picture at you! A train coming so fast that women screamed and ran out of the show! Charlie hadn't talked about anything else for months. And now he, Tom Hastings, was going to see a moving-picture show, also! No wonder he couldn't believe his ears!

"How long will it take to fix this building?" he inquired eagerly.

"Oh, it won't require much fixing," replied Mr. Rhodes, with a knowing grin. "A week or two at the most will do it!"

After that Tom wasn't a bit anxious about going to the bank. He stayed and watched the carpenters, as if watching could hurry things along. It was surprising how many other boys had the same idea.

If, in the weeks that followed, automobile riding lost some of its edge for Tom, maybe this was the reason. Late every afternoon he had to have a bath and be dressed in his Sunday clothes. Then, in the evening, he went for a ride in the Pierce Arrow. But he couldn't go without the bath and the Sunday clothes. Anything might happen when you were out for a ride. The car might break down. You might not get home for hours, all night, even. You had to be prepared, so Mother said. In some ways automobile riding was a nuisance.

But watching a building being made ready for a moving-picture show was another matter! You could do that in overalls, when you got a minute off from weeding the garden, or running errands, or helping Martin in the barn. Almost overnight Tom and Mr. Rhodes were the best of friends.

"Maggie arrived yesterday," announced Mr. Rhodes one morning, "but she isn't unpacked yet."

"Maggie? Who's Maggie?" demanded Tom.

"The moving-picture machine! It's a magniscope, isn't it, which magnifies a picture to many times its actual size? So I call her Maggie."

Instantly Tom began to insist that he was very good at unpacking, but Mr. Rhodes for some reason immediately changed the subject.

"Do you know what is done to a horse when its picture is taken for a moving picture?" he asked. "It's painted with green paint — in places, I mean — so the shadows will show up right. If you want to change a good horse into an old nag, use some green paint, also."

Tom insisted that his mother would call that "a tall tale," but Mr. Rhodes insisted that it was true. He had seen it with his own eyes. Anyway, by night, Pinkie had the news spread all over town.

Now the front of the old store building was completely changed. In the center was a boxlike ticket booth. Several feet back on either side big double doors led into the interior. Across the front stretched a sign which said BEE. Tom couldn't see any sense in that name until Mr. Rhodes hoped that people would be as busy as bees coming to see his pictures. Then Tom caught on.

Inside the building there wasn't much to be done. All the windows were boarded up so that you couldn't see a thing unless the lights were lighted. Everything was cleared out, the floor was scrubbed, and a hundred folding chairs were piled up along the walls, waiting for the first show. There were some sawhorses, too, with planks to put across them in case there weren't enough chairs. The boys could sit on the planks.

Up in front was a crude stage made of rough boards. On one side was a player piano. You put a long roll of a special kind of paper, with holes punched in it, into the front of the piano. Then you pedaled up and down with your feet. The piano played, and you didn't have to put a finger to the keyboard. There was a big drum on the stage, too, all ready for action.

On the wall at the back of the stage was something which looked like a big white sheet. It didn't look important, but it was — very! It was the screen upon which the pictures would move.

Screwed to a table at the back of the room was "Maggie." The moving-picture machine looked like a big camera with a handle on the side which had to be turned by hand. As soon as the machine was set up, everything was ready.

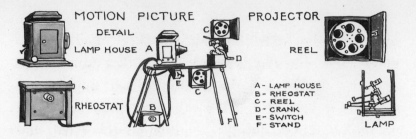

MOTION PICTURE PROJECTOR

DETAIL

LAMP HOUSE A

REEL

RHEOSTAT B

A - LAMP HOUSE
B - RHEOSTAT
C - REEL
D - CRANK
E - SWITCH
F - STAND

LAMP

Ben Gherkin

Then came the morning when the whole front of the BEE was covered with big posters:

GRAND OPENING

BEN GHERKIN

IN

THE MAGIC CORN CURE

On the largest poster of all was a picture of the funniest-looking man Pinkie had ever seen. He wore a derby hat many sizes too small, and on his upper lip was a tiny black mustache. But there was a funnier thing still. He wasn't cross-eyed. Not exactly! He was worse than cross-eyed. His two eyes turned in until he couldn't possibly see anything except his own nose — not possibly. There was a crowd of boys in front of that picture all day; and if some boy's eyes didn't turn in like Ben Gherkin's before nightfall, it wasn't because all the boys didn't try.

There were a good many mothers like Pinkie's

mother, who didn't know whether they should allow their sons and daughters to go to a nickelodeon or not. Dozens of them shook their fingers and said, in a very decided way, "Just this once and no more! Understand!" But when the great day arrived, plenty of nickels found their way through the grating of the ticket booth. Banker Hastings was there with Peggy and Pinkie, their cousins Jim Hastings and Sam White, Charlie Lane, and several more of Pinkie's particular friends.

The lights were on when the crowd entered. Sure enough, there weren't enough seats. The boys had to sit on the planks up in front. When the show was ready to begin, Mr. Rhodes went around and turned out the lights, one by one.

Now it was pitch-dark, and some boys started in making scary noises. They had never been to a moving-picture show before, and they didn't know how to behave at one. Some of the girls began to cry right out loud and said they wanted to go home. But before they could go, Mr. Rhodes lighted the two carbon lights inside "Maggie" and began to turn the handle. Something began to click steadily like a spool unwinding, and then on the screen a picture appeared — a picture that was actually moving, or rather jerking along.

There was Ben Gherkin sitting on a fence, his legs wound round each other like a corkscrew. He was still looking at his nose, only now he was funnier than ever because he was opening his mouth and talking, and you couldn't hear a word he was saying. However, if you looked at what he was doing, you could tell what he ought to be saying. It didn't take the boys a minute to figure out that he was hungry, very hungry! In fact, he was practically starving.

Now Ben was turning out his pockets. Not a cent! Poor as a church mouse! Only a big nail with a very sharp point, and on the ground a piece of string! A string and an idea!

Presently Ben was walking along, the string tied
to the nail, the nail all ready to spear. What was
this he was coming to? A grocery store with most
of the groceries on the front sidewalk! Was it a
banana he was after? No! A juicy apple? No!
Nothing but a bar of yellow soap — American
Family! If the nail speared the soap, and the
string pulled the nail and the soap along the sidewalk and up into his big coat pocket, after all it
was the nail's fault. Ben couldn't see what was
happening. He was still looking at his nose.

Jerk went the picture! Again the nail in action!
Picking up tin foil from men's cigars! Just worthless
tin foil! One piece, two, three, four! Another

jerk and Ben was cutting up soap with the nail and the string and wrapping it in tin foil.

Now what? Ben on the street corner, sitting on an old box! Ben and a big red sign!

MAGIC CORN CURE

CURE YOUR CORNS AND WALK

IN COMFORT

People were buying! Fat ladies, thin! Old men and young! Nickels were rolling into Ben's pockets!

Jerk, and along comes a crotchety old lady, thin-faced, sharp! Smelling the corn cure! Tasting it, too! Next a strolling policeman with his billy! "What's this you say, lady? No corn cure he's selling? Just soap?"

Jerk, and the chase is on! Over goes the box, and away goes Ben! In stores by the front door and out by the back! Now he's on horseback, and now he isn't! Now he's pulling off a lady's cape and wrapping it around himself! Jamming down her peach-basket hat on his head while he still keeps going!

And then — *black-out!* Something wrong with the film! Every boy in the place asking, "What's the matter?" and urging Mr. Rhodes to hurry!

Jerk, and the picture is on once more! There goes Ben straight into a very fat man with a tray

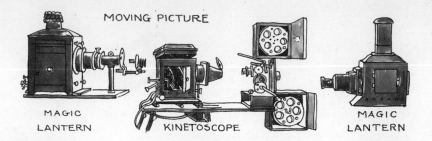

MOVING PICTURE

MAGIC LANTERN   KINETOSCOPE   MAGIC LANTERN

of custard pies! Custard pie all over Ben's face!
Then the policeman's billy hitting Ben on the
head! Captured at last! Black-out for Ben!

Once again a jerk and the policeman is giving
back the nickels. And here is Ben, sweeping out
the grocery store to pay for the soap. Out the
front door whirls the dust! The broom drops!
Ben leans over to pick it up! Under the broom
handle — something shining! Money — a silver
dollar in a crack in the sidewalk! Lucky Ben!

A final jerk and here is Ben with a big platter
of meat and potatoes. Now he isn't looking at his
nose. He is looking at the meat, and the show is
over.

If all this time the player piano had been playing
and the rat-a-tat-tat of the drum had been helping
the chase along, not a boy had even noticed it.
How could he when such things were happening
to Ben?

Now the player piano began playing "Sweet
Adeline," and Mr. Rhodes, with a magic lantern,

was throwing some slides on the screen. The boys couldn't be bothered looking at slides after having seen a real moving picture. So they spent the time laughing themselves sick over Ben until "Sweet Adeline" was over.

Twenty minutes — that's how long the picture show lasted. If it hadn't been for the black-out, it would have been over in fifteen.

"Maggie is a wonderful machine, Frank," chuckled Grandfather, on the way out, "yet I hate to think that I laughed as hard as I did at anything so foolish. Remember what I said about improving pictures!" But Tom and Charlie and the rest of the boys didn't think the picture could possibly be improved — not possibly!

Maybe Pinkie's mother and the rest of the mothers did worry for fear the picture might not be the kind of picture they would want their sons and daughters to see. But what if they had known this? If the film had come a fraction of an inch too near the carbon lamps in the picture machine, the film would have burst into flames and set the whole place on fire. The mothers hadn't inquired about such things, and they didn't know. No doubt Mr. Rhodes knew, but he trusted that everything would be all right as long as he was very careful.

Evidently Mr. Rhodes was very careful because Pinkie and the other boys saw many pictures during the coming weeks, and nothing happened. They enjoyed the pictures, every one, but Pinkie's favorite continued to be BEN GHERKIN IN THE MAGIC CORN CURE.

Model T

Young Dan Cutter opened the back door onto the ivy-covered veranda of his father's old house on Maple Avenue and looked anxiously up at the sky. It had been raining all night, a slow, continuous drizzle. Now a watery-looking sun, without much promise, was breaking through the thin, gray clouds.

Inside the house his father, Old Dan Cutter, crusty and contrary, was complaining as usual to Dan's young wife.

"So he's running around with the 'automobile set' these days! As wild a crew of money spenders as ever lived! Joined the Screwdrivers' Club, I hear, and now he's out to win the Reliability Race! If you don't put a stop to such goings on, Mary, you will end up in the poorhouse, the two of you! Mark my words! I know what I'm talking about."

"And if we do, you'll be the first one to get us out again," said gray-eyed Mary lightly, with a lilt in her voice, as she turned to take the coffeepot from the gas range behind her. "Here, now, drink your morning cup of coffee, and you'll feel better."

Ever since young Dan's mother had died two years ago and Dan and Mary had moved in to take

SINK   ICEBOX   STOVE

care of Old Dan, as everyone called him, Mary had resolved not to let his crustiness get on her nerves. At times she forgot, but she remembered often enough to make Old Dan think that there was no one in the world like Mary.

"Now, see here," she said pleasantly, but with a note of downright directness in her voice as Old Dan sipped the steaming-hot coffee. "Suppose we drive a bargain, you and I. Dan gave up his bicycle shop to take over your cigar business because you wanted him to, didn't he?"

"He did," agreed Old Dan. "Gave up a poor business for a better one!"

"Remember this," Mary went on, shaking her finger to emphasize her words. "You can change a man's business, but you can't change what's inside his head. Dan's a mechanic, and he always will be. He'll not only own a car, he'll make cars one of these days. Now, if I make him stick to the cigar store, you'll have to agree to let him tinker around with automobiles to his heart's content, once his day's work is over. How is that for a bargain?"

"No bargain at all," grumbled Old Dan. "I won't hear to it." Yet the ghost of a smile in his sharp blue eyes made Mary know that she had won the day.

"I'm going out to look the car over, Mary," called Dan from the back porch. "The rain is over, and the race is on. Call me when breakfast is ready."

The screen door flew open. Before Dan reached the bottom step, Mary had him by the arm.

"Oh, no, you don't!" she said with determination. "Get in here! Once you set your eyes on that car, I can call from now until kingdom come."

"Aw, now, Mary," coaxed Dan, but in he went.

"Coming to see me off, Father?" he asked, as he sat down at the table.

"Coming to see you off!" grunted Old Dan in disgust. "I wouldn't be caught dead there! Wasting time and good money!" Then he pushed back his chair and went out to hoe his garden.

Another second and Dan's plate was pushed back, also. "Come on, Mary, help me get started," he called gaily; and away they went together, down the long brick walk to the old barn.

THROTTLE

SPARK

STEERING
WHEEL

RADIATOR

MODEL T FORD

There stood the brand-new Model T Ford, swung high above the ground like a buggy, brass shining, and not a speck of dust to mar its polish. Of course, it was black. Hadn't Mr. Ford said that any customer of his could have a car painted any color he wished, just so the color was black? Dan and Mary gazed in admiration. Dan was the youngest man in Hastings to own a motorcar, and Mary was his wife. No wonder they were as proud as two strutting peacocks!

"Hop in, Mary," urged Dan, as, crank in hand, he walked around to the front of the Model T.

Mary climbed in behind the wheel; and then, with her heart in her throat, she sat staring at the two levers on the wheel before her. "One's the spark, one's the throttle," she kept saying over and over in her own mind. "Oh, why doesn't Dan do this himself?"

"Ten minutes to three!" called Dan, as he prepared to crank.

Mary moved the spark lever and the throttle lever until they were in exactly the position of clock hands at ten minutes to three.

Now Dan slipped the forefinger of his left hand through the loop of wire at the front of the car, which controlled the choke. He pulled on the loop, turned the crank mightily with his right hand, and soon the engine gave a welcome roar.

"Twenty-five to two!" he shouted.

Again Mary fixed the levers. Then, with a gasp of relief, she bolted from the car door while Dan leaped into her place behind the wheel.

Quickly his eye took in the three pedals at his feet. One the reverse, one the speed pedal, and one the brake. Now his foot was pressing down on the reverse pedal. He was off, backing slowly down the cinder drive. There wasn't a better car made than his Model T.

"Good-by! I'm off!" he cried exultantly.

"Good luck!" shouted Mary above the roar of the engine, but Old Dan went on with his hoeing and never even looked up.

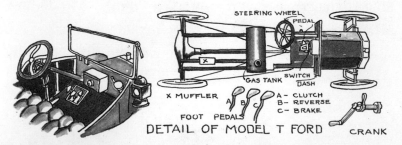

DETAIL OF MODEL T FORD

Screwdrivers' Club

In the meantime, all over town, other members of the Screwdrivers' Club were having a busy time.

A few blocks down the street from Old Dan Cutter's, Samuel White and young Sam were busy with the Stanley Steamer. At the moment Mr. White was making his own acetylene gas. It was cheaper that way. You bought a big piece of carbide for fifty cents and put it into the tank. Then you opened a valve and let water drip slowly down. The water dripping on the carbide formed the gas.

The Stanley Steamer had a boiler a little like an engine boiler with a small gasoline stove underneath to heat the water. Once the steam was up, the car would run, but not before.

"Why monkey with a newfangled gas engine when a tried and true steam engine will do the work?" argued Mr. White to himself, when it had come time to buy a car. That's the reason he had ended up by buying a Stanley Steamer.

In the carriage house next door, Mr. James Hastings, the merchant, was explaining to a very disappointed Jim that there was no use entering their Electric in a Reliability Race. You couldn't

venture out of town in an Electric. You had to stay where you could get the battery charged.

Time went by, and over on the corner of River Street and Island Avenue a strange collection of cars began to gather. Town cars, touring cars, and runabouts! A Maxwell, an Overland, a Rambler, a Peerless, and a Stanley Steamer! A Pierce Arrow, a Rolls Royce, an Oldsmobile, a Franklin, and a Ford! Even a Bulldog, and a Brush with big buggy wheels and wire spokes! There they were, with their owners in dusters and goggles beside them, while admiring wives and daughters stood round to cheer the getaway.

Of course, if any man had a son ten years old or older, like Pinkie Hastings, that son was there in duster and goggles, also. If a man didn't have a son, he usually had another man with him to help in case he needed rocks to put behind the back wheels to hold the car on a hill, or things like that. Only Dan Cutter was all alone, and young Bill Turner in his Oldsmobile.

"Young bloods with more courage than sense," said Mr. Page to Mr. Eddy on the seat beside him. "Neither one of them has as much as one spare tire, and I have six."

"All right, men," Mr. Lane, the president of the Screwdrivers' Club, called at last. "Twenty-two miles to the town square at Windfield and back again! Choose your own roads, and the driver who returns first with the fewest punctures and blow-outs and the least engine trouble wins the race. There'll be a blue ribbon to put on his windshield, if he has one. Otherwise, he can pin it to the seat to wave in the breeze. Crank your cars and get ready."

Within the next five minutes the roar of sixteen starting engines and the horrible smell of gasoline filled the air. Sixteen horns resounded with sixteen different honks. Waves and cheers and good-bys, and the cars chugged slowly forward, following the gravel road north along the river.

Four miles of gravel, then a dirt road! A dirt road after a night of drizzling rain! Already the Overland had had a blowout which sent the gravel shooting skyward. Now the Rambler was stuck in the first mud puddle it had come to. Charlie Lane at his father's side in the first car, the Rolls Royce, grinned triumphantly back at Pinkie in the second. A Pierce Arrow may be a good car, but a Rolls Royce was a foreign make, and that was better. Charlie knew who would win the race. "Chug-chug! Chug-spurt-chug!" went the cars through the mud. Before long Mr. Lake was giving his Franklin a new spark plug. The Stanley Steamer acted as if it were going to blow up until Mr. White stopped by the side of the road, and young Sam went into a farmhouse for more water.

Mr. Bill Turner in his Oldsmobile, taking every mud puddle with a splash, swung into the lead, singing at the top of his voice:

> "Come ride with me, Lucile,
> In my Merry Oldsmobile."

Bill's father had once been the crack engineer on the *Prairie Flyer*, the finest engine on the Hastings,

Lake Shore, and Western Railroad. Bill was an engineer, too, only on his days off he had the "motorcar bug." Maybe being an engineer helped him to become the best automobile driver in Hastings. Anyway, he was.

Now the cars had come to a fork in the road. All the sensible drivers chose the longer, lower road which skirted the river. The more daring ones took the higher, shorter road, even though they knew that Snake Hill lay straight in their

path. Away they went, the Rolls Royce, the Pierce Arrow, the Oldsmobile, and the Model T, with the Oldsmobile still in the lead.

> "Down the road of life we'll fly,
> Automobubbling you and I,"

warbled Big Bill Turner. Charlie Lane, disgusted to think that the Rolls Royce couldn't keep the lead, wished he would stop that singing. That's what made the Olds go faster.

Snake Hill

Now, straight ahead of the cars, loomed the road up Snake Hill, long, narrow, winding, steep, rocky, muddy, and everything else that could make a road a hazard.

"Thank goodness for this big car and its powerful engine!" breathed Mr. Lane with a half-worried, half-satisfied expression on his face.

"We're fools, just plain fools, to risk good cars on a hill like this," thought Mr. Hastings.

"Come on, Model T, show what you are good for!" urged Dan Cutter, as if he were talking to his best friend.

Big Bill Turner, far up the road, almost to the foot of the hill, went on warbling:

"To the church we'll quickly steal,
Then the wedding bells will peal."

Suddenly, to everyone's surprise, the Oldsmobile stopped.

"Engine went dead at the very sight of the hill," boasted Charlie Lane triumphantly.

But the engine wasn't dead, not a bit of it. Bill was turning around. That's what he was doing. Turning round in that narrow, rocky road!

OLDSMOBILE   1910   ROLLS ROYCE

Mr. Lane, fearing that the Rolls Royce would gain upon Bill before the turn was completed, took his foot from the gas. He shouldn't have done that. Bill had that car turned round before the Rolls Royce was a hundred yards away.

"Now what's he going to do?" complained Mr. Lane to Charlie. "Two cars can't pass in a narrow road like this."

"He's giving up and going home! His car's no good!" grinned Charlie in delight.

But Bill wasn't going home. He didn't want to pass. He had never even thought of it. He just went on warbling:

"You can go as far as you like with me,
In my Merry Oldsmobile."

Then he started to back, actually back up that hill! What on earth was he thinking of?

"When you haven't a powerful engine, you have to do strange things," chuckled Mr. Lane, recovering from his astonishment enough to talk.

Chug, chug, chug went the Oldsmobile, onward and upward. Chug, chug over the rocks and bumps and chug around the tree trunks, while Bill, craning his neck from the car, guided it by looking backward.

Forward to take the hill at high speed went the brave Rolls Royce. Perhaps Mr. Lane forgot that he had taken his foot from the gas when he had seen the turning car in the road ahead. Perhaps the big Rolls Royce didn't have a good running start for that hill. Or it may have been that Mr. Lane was so afraid of overtaking that singing Oldsmobile on the way up that he reached for the brake every once in a while. Anyway, before many minutes the Rolls Royce was coughing and choking. More gas! Still the car coughed! Desperately Mr. Lane shifted to second speed! Too late! The engine died; and though Mr. Lane pulled hard on the hand brake, the minute he took his foot from the foot brake, the big car started rolling backward down the long hill.

"Get out, Charlie, quick! Get some rocks, the biggest ones you can find, to put under the back

SPARK→
THROTTLE

RADIATOR

STEERING
WHEEL

PIERCE ARROW 1910

GEARS
BRAKES

wheels," he ordered, and out jumped Charlie into the mud.

Meanwhile, Mr. Hastings, with an anxious eye on the trouble ahead, stopped his car at the foot of the hill.

"Too bad, Tom," he said. "We can't pass that car on the hill, and we can't risk having it back into us. We may as well do what we can to help."

"And lose the race!" stormed Pinkie, as he jumped out into the mud, also, and started in Charlie's direction.

Pinkie started in immediately telling Charlie to get that old car out of the way and not to lose the race for a good car. Charlie immediately retorted that a Pierce Arrow couldn't win a race if there weren't a Rolls Royce in the world. It looked as if they would end up by throwing rocks at each other instead of putting them under the wheels of the car.

Honk! Honk! "Watch out!" shouted Mr. Hastings, as a Model T Ford squirmed past them.

It missed the ditch by inches and went up the hill in low. Of course it did! A Model T could sidle in and out where no other car would think of going.

"Now see!" called Mr. Hastings. "Stop your quarreling and hurry up here. There're an Oldsmobile and a Model T ahead of us now; and if they don't have a dozen punctures, the race is won already."

After that Pinkie and Charlie worked together like long-lost brothers.

When the big Rolls Royce was propped up at last, Mr. Lane got out in the mud and cranked. Soon the two big cars were chugging up the hill in low. Ahead of them Dan Cutter was praying under his breath that he wouldn't burn out his low-speed gear before he reached the hilltop.

"I'll tell you a secret, Charlie," smiled Mr. Lane, when at last Snake Hill was behind them. "There's a short cut up ahead. I've taken it many times in the surrey. It leads through a strip of woodland and straight into Windfield. Not one of these other drivers will think of it, I'm certain. We'll make up for lost time and win the race yet."

"Hurrah, boys!" shouted Charlie exultantly. A few minutes later he carelessly waved Pinkie for-

ward, as the Pierce Arrow honked and passed them by. "Go right ahead!" he called. "We'll beat you yet!"

In a short time Mr. Lane turned the nose of the car into a side road. He should have remembered what a road through a wood would be like after a night of rain. Perhaps he did, but his mind was on speed, not mud. Anyway, not ten minutes later the Rolls Royce was hopelessly sunk in the mud in the middle of the woods. Two hours later Mr. Lane and Charlie were still hunting for a good-natured farmer who didn't hate motorcars and would lend them a good strong team of horses.

Tinkering

All this time things were going well with the Pierce Arrow, very well, indeed. The radiator had begun to boil on the long pull uphill; but Mr. Hastings had slowed down a bit, and now everything seemed to be all right.

Before long Pinkie sighted the Model T by the side of the road. Dan Cutter was dipping an inner tube in the puddle of water, looking for the hole. Dan looked up and grinned as they flew by.

"He's safe for the next half hour!" asserted Mr. Hastings confidently. "But I can't imagine what has happened to that Rolls Royce."

On went the Pierce Arrow; and just as the Hastings rounded a curve with Windfield in the near distance, they heard one loud pop and then another. Then the whistling sound of escaping air! The next instant they saw the Oldsmobile headed toward them, careening over to the side of the road with not one puncture, but two.

"Still backing?" grinned Mr. Hastings, with a glint in his eye.

"Backing nothing!" shouted Big Bill. "I'm on my way home to claim that blue ribbon."

"We'll see you on our way back," called Pinkie.

"Oh, no, you won't," shouted Big Bill, as he set to work in desperation.

"He's settled for a while," grinned Mr. Hastings, looking triumphantly out of the corner of his eye at Pinkie. "I believe we're going to win the race, son. I really believe we are."

Now the Pierce Arrow was rolling along over the pavement of Windfield. Mr. Hastings stopped long enough at the town square to give his name to the man who was waiting there and immediately headed the car toward home.

"Second car in!" said the man admiringly. "Not a mite of engine trouble? Not even a puncture? If you can only overtake that singing Oldsmobile, you'll win the race yet."

"We'll overtake it all right!" boasted Mr. Hastings. "We left the driver back there on the road with two punctures and no spare tires."

Mr. Hastings was right. They did overtake the Oldsmobile with Bill Turner pumping up a tire at fever heat. A moment later the Model T, on its way to Windfield, passed with a friendly honk.

Time went by. On a long stretch of rough road Mr. Hastings shifted to second speed, the engine heated, the water in the radiator began to boil once more, and going slowly didn't stop it.

"Pshaw! This is the second time this has happened," said Mr. Hastings with a discouraged headshake. "We'll have to stop for water, Tom, and give the engine time to cool off."

He stopped the Pierce Arrow at a farmyard gate, and Tom went bounding away up a long, long lane. Why did it have to be Pinkie who went for that pail of water? Why are boys always sent on errands that men don't want to do themselves? It would have been much better if Mr. Hastings had not been left alone with that car.

The minute Pinkie was gone, Mr. Hastings took off the radiator cap to let the water cool down more quickly. He burned his fingers a little on the cap. It would have been a fortunate thing if he had burned them a little more. Then he wouldn't have felt the urge to lift the hood and begin tinkering. He really didn't do much, but he tested the spark plugs, tightened a bolt here, found a loose wire there, and monkeyed around in general. He certainly did get a thrill out of an engine.

"What's the matter!" asked Pinkie, coming back on the run and splashing water all about him.

"Nothing at all!" insisted Mr. Hastings. He put down the hood, added water gradually to the radiator, climbed into the seat while Pinkie ran back with the pail, and soon they were off. The Model T and the Oldsmobile were still behind them, and the Rolls Royce—nobody knew where.

"You weren't tinkering with this car, were you?" asked Pinkie, as they rolled along. "Remember, Mr. Samson said that you wouldn't have trouble unless you began to tinker."

"I know what I'm doing," answered Mr. Hastings crossly. Perhaps that reminder about Mr. Samson gave him a guilty feeling. Anyway, Tom had sense enough to change the subject.

"I wish there were a song for this car," he sighed regretfully. "Then we could sing it when we get the blue ribbon."

Just as he said that, the car gave a little cough and began to slow down. Another cough! Slower still! While the looks of consternation on the faces of Pinkie and Mr. Hastings grew greater and greater, the Pierce Arrow stopped.

"Out of gas!" asserted Mr. Hastings, as he hopped out, pushed aside the front seat, and used the ruler. The tank was half full of gas.

Now Mr. Hastings was worried. Crank as he would, the engine would not start. When Pinkie insisted mournfully, "You did, too, tinker! You did, too! Now see what you've done!" Mr. Hastings was so angry and disgusted with himself that he almost gave Pinkie a good sound slap. Again he lifted the hood, but this time he didn't tinker. He just looked. While he was looking, the Oldsmobile went sailing by, and not long afterward the sturdy Model T Ford honked merrily.

In the meantime, Pinkie was sitting on a stone by the roadside, utterly disconsolate. By the time Mr. Hastings put down the hood and tried the crank again, only to fail once more, he was much sorrier for Tom than he was for himself.

"Never mind, son!" he urged, sitting down beside Pinkie on the stone. "It's all my fault, I know. But someday we'll win a race, you and I together. I won't tinker the next time, Tom. I promise you I won't."

After that Pinkie felt better, though the disappointed tears still came in spite of all he could do. Now his father and he talked things over together.

Maybe Mr. Hastings hadn't done anything to that car. Maybe it would have stopped anyway. If some part had to be replaced, there would be nothing to do but send down East after it. That was the trouble with newfangled things like motorcars. Only the original makers carried the parts. If it wasn't a part, but some other thing that was the matter, Mr. Samson might have to come to Hastings to fix it. All Pinkie and his father could do was to keep an eye out for a team of horses and a wagon to tow them back home. Tom saw how it was, didn't he? Mr. Hastings hoped that he did.

Yes, Tom saw how it was. But why did it have to be a hay wagon that came by? Why did it have to be that? To his dying day Tom would never forget how it felt to come home to Hastings in a splendid Pierce Arrow pulled by an old hay wagon.

Blue Ribbon or Red

All this time the Model T and the singing Oldsmobile went bravely on. Not without trouble, of course! The Oldsmobile, with punctures in each of the other two tires, fell back into second place. But punctures were nothing compared to what happened to the Model T.

Dan Cutter had come up Snake Hill for the first time that morning. He had never gone down. In fact, he had never gone down any hills which amounted to anything. He didn't know anything about hills. He just had courage.

Dan was expecting speed, but he never expected the amount of speed that car picked up on the way downhill. He had to keep his foot on the brake pedal almost every second. Even that wasn't enough. It took the hand brake, also. But by using the two together, he was able to take the hill in slow and sensible fashion, the way a hill should be taken. Not the way Bill Turner was taking it! At a place where the road separated for a time and ran on either side of a big tree, Bill actually raced by, actually raced.

"Watch out for your — !" Bill shouted. But what Dan was to watch out for, he didn't know.

A few minutes later Dan began to sniff and sniff again. Something was burning. Someone must be burning rubbish. He glanced back as he passed a tree stump. Was that a whiff of smoke? Perhaps a tramp had a fire in a field nearby.

But by the time Dan reached the foot of the hill, it was plain to be seen that the smoke didn't come from rubbish nor from a tramp's fire. It came from the wheels of the Model T.

"You're on fire! Get that 'devil wagon' away from here before you burn my fence!" shouted the irate farmer, running out with a pail of water for the fence but not for the wheels.

Dan took his foot from the brake. The car shot forward under its own momentum, gradually slowed down, and the engine sputtered and died of its own accord. Then Dan had to carry water for his own wheels. In a few minutes the smoke was gone, and a sadder and wiser driver cranked the Ford and jumped in behind the wheel. He tried the brakes. They didn't hold worth a cent. Burned out, both of them! Why had he ever entered this race? Now he'd have to crawl home.

Crawl home is what Dan did — but not for long. Instantly he began experimenting with a very important question. How do you stop a Model T Ford without brakes? How do you?

By the time Dan drove up to the starting place, he knew the answer. He stopped without a speck of trouble. No one would have known what had happened if he had not told the judges.

Of course, the singing Oldsmobile was there before him with only four punctures chalked up against its record. Four punctures against one puncture, slower time, and burned-out brakes. If Bill Turner warbled louder than ever as he fastened the blue ribbon to his windshield, Dan didn't mind much, particularly since Mary didn't seem to notice that the ribbon the judges gave Dan was red, not blue. Mary was too busy calling attention to something else.

"Look!" urged Mary. "Quick, Dan, look!"

There, disappearing round a street corner, was Old Dan Cutter.

"He came to see you win," whispered Mary, "but he doesn't want you to see him. Oh, *no!*"

That night, when everyone else was supposed to be in bed, Dan sat on the veranda thinking. The door behind him opened softly. He turned to find his father putting something into his hand.

"Use this to buy a good car," grunted Old Dan, "and the next time you go into a race, win it!"

Dan grinned a delighted grin. "Keep your money!" he said, his pleasure showing in his voice. "Whether I won that race or whether I didn't, there isn't a more reliable car made than my Model T. I can count on it in any emergency. Even if I burn out the brakes, the reverse pedal will stop the car. I found that out for myself today."

"Humph!" grunted Old Dan. "Seems like it might be a handy thing to remember. Glad to hear that you're going to bed tonight a wiser man than you were this morning."

And young Dan thought he heard an amused chuckle, as Old Dan went off to bed.

A Tale and a Discovery

Down at the bend in the riverbank where Indian Creek flowed into the Big Turtle River, Pinkie and Sam and Jim were angling for red horses and bullheads, hoping to catch a bass. Indian Creek was overhung with willows and bordered with drooping grasses, a good fishing spot on a showery Saturday afternoon.

On the top rail of the horse-lot fence nearby sat Charlie. First he took a bite of doughnut, then a bite of cooky. Every once in a while he dropped a bite down the throat of his bulldog,

Spunk, who clung to the fence post beside him.
If Charlie was feeling good, who could blame him?

The boys were listening to a thrilling tale while
waiting for a bass to bite.

"There we stood by that stretch of track,"
Pinkie was saying, "in the boiling-hot sun. Mr.
Gates was complaining like everything. Couldn't
we have any mercy on an old man? Wasn't he
perfectly willing to take my father's word for what
happened? Couldn't he read the train reports?
But my father just laughed and held the big black
umbrella farther down over his head. Mr. Gates
had been asking for an engine that could go ninety

BASS   RED HORSE   BULLHEAD

miles an hour, for ever so long. Now he was going to get it. Not through train reports, either! He was going to see it with his own eyes. So we stood patiently waiting. It was terrible. Then far off we could see something coming. Nearer, nearer, nearer, nearer! Suddenly a train went whizzing by — whizzing — and that was all."

"All!" exclaimed Charlie, who didn't think much of stories that turned out in that fashion. "Just an old train flying by! I don't care if I wasn't there!"

"Aw, listen to him talk!" retorted Pinkie. "The trouble with him is he hasn't any imagination. That train was going ninety-nine miles an hour, faster than any train in this country has ever gone before. That engine was making history, and he says he didn't even want to see it!"

Charlie looked a bit shamefaced. He hadn't thought about the history. "What was the name of that engine, anyway?" he asked next.

"It didn't have a name yesterday," explained Pinkie, "just a number — 99. But now it has. Mr. Gates calls it *Big Tom* after my father, who helped to design it. He says he wouldn't think of asking for an engine that could go one hundred fifty miles an hour; or as sure as he was born, my father would set to work to build it. He says he'll have to find a different way of sharpening the wits of his chief engineer from now on."

"Think of having an engine called after you!" exclaimed Sam. "Will *Big Tom* always go ninety-nine miles an hour?"

"Probably never again after yesterday," explained Pinkie. "It wouldn't be safe. My father just wanted to show Mr. Gates that it could be done. That's all!"

Maybe it was the showery afternoon. Maybe the fish swam up to hear the story. Anyway, before long, the boys had half a dozen bullheads, small, not much to look at, but still fish. Now what to do with them was the question!

There wasn't a mite of use taking them to Ellen at Pinkie's house. She would throw up her hands, at least, if she didn't throw the boys and the fish, too, out of her kitchen. It would be the same way at Sam's house, or at Jim's or Charlie's. Pinkie

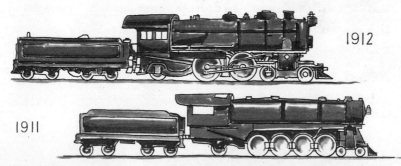

1912

1911

couldn't even depend upon Grandmother at a time like this. Grandmother couldn't abide bullheads.

Of course, the boys could have cleaned and cooked the fish themselves. But it was a lazy day, and hot and showery, and a few other things; and the boys didn't feel like doing it. Still, you can't throw a good catch of fish away.

"William!" exclaimed Sam at last; and, "Smart boy!" exclaimed the others.

Certainly it was William! He might be serious-minded and smile very seldom. But you could depend upon William to do the things no one else wanted to do for you, such as mending your dog's broken leg instead of trying to persuade you to put him out of his misery, and things like that.

William lived in a little cottage out on the Old Coach Road at the edge of town. He generally gave up scissors-grinding at about four in the afternoon to work for a while in his garden. He would welcome a good fish for his supper.

The boys followed along the bank of the creek under the willows, then took a short cut through the east end of town to the Old Coach Road. There, amid the ruts and mud, much to their surprise, they found some men working.

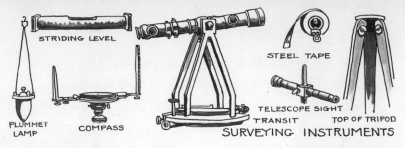

STRIDING LEVEL

STEEL TAPE

TELESCOPE SIGHT

TRANSIT

TOP OF TRIPOD

PLUMMET LAMP

COMPASS

SURVEYING INSTRUMENTS

Surveyors, that's what they were! One man had a surveyor's instrument mounted on a tripod. He was looking through it, sighting something, no doubt, and calling directions to another man who was making measurements with a cord stretched along the ground.

The boys stopped in their tracks for just one second. What was going on here? Then their bump of curiosity carried them straight forward in the direction of the tripod.

"What's that for? What are you doing?" they asked gingerly. You see, there are two kinds of men in the world, and the boys had had experience with both kinds. That is why they asked gingerly, feeling their way.

There is the kind of man who would have said, "Hello, fisherman! How much does that black bass weigh?" All the time he would have gone right on with his work. Then, if the boys had repeated, as they surely would have repeated, "What's that for? May we have a look?" he would have answered, "Can't be bothered now, fellows!

If you want to hang around until I'm through, something might be done about it. But clear out of my way now! Scat!" Then the boys would have cleared, and waited, and understood.

The other kind of man thinks a boy hasn't any excuse for living. He may amount to something once he's grown to be a man; but as long as he's a boy, he's a nuisance.

Unfortunately, the surveyors were the second kind of men. So the boys didn't find out anything, and they didn't stay long. When they asked William whether he knew what those men were doing, he said of course he did. Maybe that was why the boys were so willing to follow William's suggestion.

"My old mouser hasn't had a feast like that in a month of Sundays," he said, after one look at the bullheads. "It won't take her a second to get rid of those fish."

If the boys were a bit disappointed in William when he inferred that their fish were fit only for a cat, they didn't show it. The cat got the fish, and the boys sat down to hear the story.

GRINDING STONES

Old Coach Road

"We're going to pave the Old Coach Road. For a full four miles out into the country, we're going to pave it," William began.

"Pave it! What for?" demanded Pinkie. Pavement was for cities. The idea of pavement reaching away out into the country where scarcely anyone lived, pavement without a house or building on either side of it, seemed perfectly ridiculous.

"To keep from sending good money after bad, that's why!" answered William. Then, as the boys looked completely mystified, he went on.

"You see, it's this way. Every time it rains, that Old Coach Road and all the other roads like it get full of ruts and holes. Farmers can't get to town with their milk and butter and eggs without danger of breaking their horses' legs or getting stuck in the mud. So the Highway Commissioners — they're the men we elect to take care of the roads — get their men and teams together and haul gravel to fill the ruts. That costs money. Costs me money, costs your fathers money, and every man who owns property. We have to pay a road tax to keep up the roads.

"No sooner are the roads fixed than, sure as

tunket, it begins to rain once more, or the snow melts, or the frost heaves up the roads into hills and hollows. Then work has to begin all over again. Sending good money after bad, I call it. And even at best, if we haven't got mud and holes, we've got dust. See how it works out?"

Of course the boys saw how it worked out. By the time they reached home, they thought all the roads in all the country round should be paved. Why stop with the Old Coach Road? Pinkie even suggested that idea to his father as the family set out for a ride that evening on their safety bicycles, Father and Tom in knickers, Peggy in bloomers, and Mother in her new divided skirt.

Mr. Hastings looked simply disgusted. "Really, Tom, if you have a head, why not use it? How much do you think that four miles of paved road is going to cost? Thirty thousand dollars! Now do you want to go on paving every road that comes into Hastings?"

No, Tom didn't. He didn't want to pave even the rocky patch which gave him a spill from his bicycle as they rounded the next corner. Thirty thousand dollars! There was something to be said for dirt roads, after all. No hard road was worth that much money.

"Yes, Tom, it is," said his mother, as she rode along beside him. "The better the roads are leading into Hastings, the more the farmers will come to town. The more the farmers come, the more they will trade with the merchants, and the more money the merchants will make. You see that, don't you?"

Mrs. Hastings paused, and Mr. Hastings went on. "The more money the merchants make, the richer and more successful the city will become, the better schools and parks and buildings we can have, and the more other people will want to make their homes here. Come, Tom, you're old enough to be intelligent in matters like this."

Certainly Tom was intelligent. He saw how it was. But thirty thousand dollars!

"Well, it isn't as bad as it looks," laughed Mr. Hastings. "The State is going to help us out. Maybe you don't know it, Tom, but this state we are living in is divided up into big sections of land, called townships. A township is made up of cities and towns and farm lands. Every person who owns property in a township pays taxes on that property. Some of the tax money goes to the State to pay the expenses of running the State. Some goes to the township to pay for building and repairing bridges and roads and things like that.

Some of the tax money, paid by people in towns and cities like Hastings, goes to pay the expenses of running the towns and cities.

"And now, to make a long story short, what do you suppose the State proposes to do? If any township will put in a stretch of hard road, the State will give back to that township enough tax money to pay one-third the cost of laying the road. That will help a lot. Of course, we'll have to raise our own road tax to pay the rest, but we figure a hard road will be worth it."

Tom may not have quite understood all his father was talking about, but one idea was perfectly clear. If other places were to have hard roads, Hastings was, too. Have them and have them first! Choosing the Old Coach Road as the first road to be paved was no mistake, either. Wasn't it the most widely traveled road in all the country round?

"You're right about that," said his mother with a smile. "The Old Coach Road began bringing settlers to Hastings as far back as that long-ago day when your great-grandfather drove over it in a covered wagon. It has continued to bring newcomers through all the intervening years."

Later that evening, as Pinkie and his father put the bicycles away in the carriage house, Mr. Hastings waited for Tom to close the door.

"Hard roads won't come overnight, Tom," he said in a thoughtful, serious voice. "The cost is too great. But someday, when you are a man, the towns and rich farm lands round about may be joined to a bigger and better Hastings by a whole series of hard roads. Who can tell?"

Tom's eyes lighted with interest as his father went on. "When that day comes, 'twill be interesting to recall that those hard roads had their beginnings in the measurements of the surveyors you saw this afternoon."

Shovelers All

During the following days, the *Evening Herald* was full of articles about the new road. Serious articles, all of them! How much would the road cost, and why? What was it to be made of? When was the actual work to begin? Even the conversation of men on the street corners took on a serious tone as they talked of the big undertaking.

It wasn't until Mr. Spencer, the hardware merchant, and Mr. Page, who kept a big department store, got their heads together that the seriousness turned to amused laughter, and laughter to pleased anticipation.

"It's going to take a sight of digging, Frank, to level off that Old Coach Road when the time comes," said Mr. Page one hot August morning, as he strolled into the hardware store. "Seems like we ought not to have to pay for all of it. Seems like it might be a fine thing to get some of the Big Ones who've been wanting this road for ever so long to do some of the digging. How does that idea strike you?"

"Strike me! I don't know what you are talking about. Has the heat gone to your head?" inquired Mr. Spencer.

"No, my head's cool enough!" replied Mr. Page. "But some of these Big Fellows need exercise to keep them healthy. Take the governor of this state, for instance. What does he know about digging? And Tom Hastings, who sits in a railroad office from one year's end to another! How long has it been since he's lifted a shovel full of dirt? And Charlie Lane, who runs a woolen mill from his chair in front of a roll-top desk! Do you think he knows anything about work? These fellows ought to have a chance to show what they are good for. Now, it occurred to me that if I furnished the overalls and you furnished the shovels —"

There Mr. Page stopped — stopped to give the idea time to take hold. And take hold it did.

"May I live to see the day!" exclaimed Mr. Spencer the very next second. His eyes twinkled with amused laughter. "I'll furnish the shovels, you'll furnish the overalls; and when Ben Martin gives the word, we'll all pitch in and lift a few shovels of dirt to help the good work along. Of all the ideas I ever heard tell of, this is the richest and rarest. Did you stay awake all night thinking it up?"

But good as the idea was, it took Ben Martin, the Highway Commissioner, to add salt to it.

In the midst of chuckling and grinning over his mind's-eye picture of the governor in overalls, Ben suddenly clapped both Mr. Page and Mr. Spencer on the back at the same moment.

"I'll go farther than that," he insisted. "I'll pay you for your work from the road-tax fund! As much as you're worth, and not one cent more!"

A splendid suggestion, which added the final touch to an excellent plan! But try as they would, neither Mr. Spencer nor Mr. Page could get Ben to admit how much money he stood ready to pay for their services. "As much as you're worth; not a cent more," he chuckled.

Days went by. Then news spread about town that digging on the Old Coach Road was to begin. The very next morning the Governor of the State, a certain railroad engineer, a woolen-mill owner, an old man who had been a bank president in his day, and several other important people received a strange summons, which read:

Dear Sir:

In order that you may labor willingly with your hands, as you have worked successfully with your brains; in order that you may show by such work that you believe in the cause of good roads, which will result in a better township, a richer and happier state, and a greater nation; you are summoned to appear on the Old Coach Road in the Township of Hastings at the point where the road leaves the city of Hastings, at three o'clock in the afternoon on the fifteenth of August, Nineteen Hundred and Ten. You will hold yourself in readiness to shovel dirt or to do any other work which may be found necessary. For such services, you will be paid exactly what you are worth in the lawful coin of the land.

(Signed) Ben E. Martin

Highway Commissioner

It is too bad that Mr. Spencer and Mr. Page and Mr. Martin couldn't have seen the expressions on the faces of a dozen men when they opened those letters. Yet there wasn't one among those summoned who wasn't highly amused and who didn't agree to appear without hesitation. When the story leaked out around Hastings, every one of the invited ones had to stand plenty of good-natured joking. If they didn't have good dispositions before, they had to cultivate them. But before long they began to joke one another.

"Now we'll see who's the better man!" boasted Mr. Lane, as he met Pinkie's father on his way to the train. "I've been waiting to show you up for years back."

"Show me up! Man alive, what are you talking about?" burst forth Mr. Hastings. "I'll be able to hold my job until the road is done. You'll be fired before the first hour is over."

Even Banker Hastings was thoroughly amused. "I expect to be worth a sight of money after the fifteenth of August, Tom," chuckled Grandfather. "I was never *sure* what I *was* worth. Now I'm going to find out."

But Grandfather hadn't an idea what Ben Martin was planning to do. No one had.

Great Men in Overalls

The morning of the fifteenth of August arrived, hot and muggy, very unpleasant weather, indeed, for shoveling. It hadn't rained for a week. The ground was dry and caked, and dust lay white and thick on everything.

Out on the Old Coach Road everything was in readiness. A platform had been built by the side of the road and gaily decorated with streamers of red, white, and blue. Folding chairs for the performers were piled at one end of the platform, and at the other end were a box of overalls and a dozen or more shiny new shovels. If there was an awning over the platform, that was Mr. Martin's way of keeping the workers from having a sunstroke.

"I hope those overalls are big enough," he cautioned Mr. Page, when the box was being opened. "Some of these men may swell up with pride in their own performance."

There was a crowd at the station when the governor arrived. Several other important people were with him, and Pinkie's father immediately whirled them away in the Pierce Arrow to Grandmother's house. That is the reason there was no extra place at the table for Pinkie that day.

August the fifteenth was just an ordinary working day, not a holiday by any means. Nevertheless, a goodly crowd of people had gathered long before the appointed hour. Squatted on the ground in front of the platform, where seeing was best, were Pinkie and Charlie and several of their particular friends.

Mr. Martin was master of ceremonies. It was a half-gay, half-serious occasion. Of course, the governor gave a talk. If what he said was simply a repetition of what William and Pinkie's father had already said about the importance of paved highways for Hastings, yet the fact that he believed these things, also, seemed to make them much more important. Perhaps everyone enjoyed his speech more because he didn't talk long. At the most serious moment he braced up, threw back his shoulders, and then looked in Ben Martin's direction.

"I understand I'm here for work," he said. "Where's that shovel?"

"Calm yourself, calm yourself," cautioned Ben, as he took the first pair of overalls from the box at his side.

If the overalls were much, much too big for Governor Mills, and if they looked very, very

funny on top of his splendid tailor-made clothes,
these things only added to the laughter of the
good-natured crowd. Another minute and the dirt
was flying while Ben stood by the governor's side,
timing his efforts and counting the shovelfuls.

"Time's up!" called Ben after a few minutes.

"Are these mine to keep?" asked a very red-faced governor, pointing to the overalls and the shovel and wiping the sweat from his forehead.

"They are!" laughed Ben. "Keep them as a souvenir!"

Grandfather, as the best-known and most important person in all the group upon the platform, was next in line.

"I'm a better man than you are, even if I am seventy-two," he asserted, pulling on his overalls and looking at the governor. Then he went to work for dear life.

Everyone was so interested in watching that no one paid any attention when two freckled-faced boys slipped quietly away.

Man followed man amid the laughter and cheers of the onlookers, who were continually urging each man on to greater effort. Finally a goodly strip of the Old Coach Road was dug up after some fashion or other. The last man was just reaching for his shovel when two boys gave a running jump for the back of the platform. Pinkie and Charlie — in overalls — each clutching a shovel tightly in his hand!

"I swan!" declared Ben Martin in astonishment.

"Two extra shovelers who want to break the record! Shall we give them a chance?"

"Yes, yes!" called back the laughing crowd; and if Pinkie and Charlie didn't do better than the other men on that platform, they didn't do worse.

"Ladies and gentlemen," announced Ben very solemnly, when the shoveling was over. "You can see for yourselves that with a gang of workmen as poor as these, it will be years before the Old Coach Road will be in condition to be paved. I am sure you will agree that there is nothing left to be done but to give each one his time and his walking papers and call it a day."

Then Ben took some folded papers from his pocket. If he paused for a moment to write something upon two of them, Charlie and Pinkie didn't realize how important that pause was.

"Governor Mills," Mr. Martin went on, stepping up to the governor and holding out one of the papers, "here is your check for as much as your work was worth, and no more."

EXAMPLES OF
OLD CHECKS

No. 45 ~~~~~~~ Chicago, June 22, 1897
BANK OF GRAND CROSSING
BABCOCK & LELAND
Pay to S. J. Umbreit or order
Five Hundred ——— Dollars
$500ºº
W. J. Miller

CHICAGO, Jany 10 1911— No. 446
FEDERAL TRUST & SAVINGS BANK
N E Cor La Salle and Adams Streets.
PAY TO THE ORDER OF
N. J. Orr — $100 40
One Hundred & 40/100 ——— Dollars
Thos Walton

INDORSED CHECK

323

If some of the men in that group had the idea that they were better shovelers than some others, the next few minutes were a sad disappointment. Each man, even Pinkie and Charlie, received his reward, and each check was for the same amount.

The boys jumped from the platform and raced for the shade of a tree by the roadside. Then, with all the other boys and girls crowding round, Pinkie read for all to hear.

HASTINGS NATIONAL BANK

Pay to the order of Mr. Thomas Hastings, the Fourth, one penny ($.01) in the lawful coin of this nation.

(Signed) Governor William A. Mills

So the governor, too, had had his own little joke. He, not Ben Martin, was paying the bills.

As the Pierce Arrow left for the station with the governor and the other important officials, Pinkie climbed into the surrey with Grandfather. Instead

325

of turning the horses' noses toward home, Grandfather jogged slowly out along the Old Coach Road away from Hastings.

The fun and the merriment of the day were over, and Grandfather was strangely silent as they jogged along. Then slowly he began:

"Today set me thinking, Tom, thinking of Lightning Joe and something he told me when I rode with him on the seat of the big brown stagecoach. Do you know who made this road? Buffalo! Great herds of them used to wander over these prairies, beating down grasses and bushes and even small trees as they went. Every herd that passed made this path wider and deeper."

The moment Grandfather began to talk, Tom's eyes grew big with interest and excitement.

"Then came the Indians," Grandfather went on. "Their trail followed the buffalo trail. You see, Tom, buffalo were wise. Their trails always led to the easiest passes in the hills and forests. No

INDIAN TRAILS

wonder the Indians followed where the buffalo led. And then came the road of the white man."

Grandfather stopped the surrey under a great oak tree by the roadside.

"Jump out, Tom," he said quietly. "Look closely, part way up the trunk."

Tom looked; and there, imbedded in the trunk of the great tree, he found a scar, healed over for years, but still showing.

"We found scars like that when we were boys no older than you, on certain trees that have long since disappeared," continued Grandfather. "We never knew, but we liked to believe, that the tomahawks of the Indians had blazed this trail."

Now it was Tom's turn to be thoughtful. Buffalo and Indian trails, the road of the white man and the paved highway yet to come! The old familiar road seemed a very different place as Grandfather and Tom drove home together and the sun descended over the valley of the Big Turtle.

AUTOMOBILE ROADS

Headlines

Down behind the big pressroom of the *Evening Herald*, Pinkie and Sam and Charlie and a group of other boys had their heads in a huddle. Those who could find room sat on a big packing box; and those who could not, stood hands on knees, leaning over. Their empty paper sacks hung from their shoulders. For the moment, peddling papers was out of the question.

In vain a commanding voice from the newspaper office called to them to fill their sacks and be on their way. Did they want every man, woman, and child in town calling up to find out why his newspaper was late? The boys didn't stir. They didn't have to stir. Sam White's father, the editor in chief of the *Herald*, understood how it was. Hadn't he tossed the first paper from the presses to the boys himself? There wasn't going to be a single paper delivered in Hastings that evening until the boys had had time to scan the headlines and look at the pictures.

FLYING MACHINE WILL COME

So read the headlines; and now Pinkie, in a very dramatic voice, was reading for all to hear.

Ninety-nine people out of a hundred in this city have never seen an airplane. No doubt, you who are reading this are among the ninety-nine. How will it seem to see a flying machine glide swiftly over the ground? How will you feel at the moment when it rises majestically in air, its white wings flashing and gleaming in sunlight? Will you

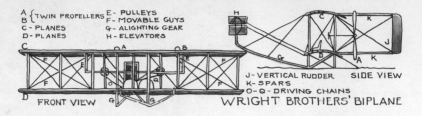

A { TWIN PROPELLERS
B {
C - PLANES
D - PLANES
E - PULLEYS
F - MOVABLE GUYS
G - ALIGHTING GEAR
H - ELEVATORS

J - VERTICAL RUDDER   SIDE VIEW
K - SPARS
O - Q - DRIVING CHAINS

FRONT VIEW   WRIGHT BROTHERS' BIPLANE

stand speechless with the wonder of it, as the great white ship sails above the roof tops of Hastings?

You will if the committee in charge can raise five thousand dollars.

"Five thousand dollars! Five thousand!" exclaimed Charlie in a voice which plainly showed that he didn't believe there was that much money in the world. *"We'll* never see an airplane at that rate, never as long as we live!"

"Aw, we will, too!" asserted Pinkie. "You're always saying that this town can't do things; and it always delivers the goods, so my father says. Just look here, fellows, look here!"

There, staring up at the boys from the center of the first page, was a picture of a queer-looking flying machine. It looked something like a box-shaped kite and not much stronger. The seat for the pilot was away out in front of the wings. It had two wings, and the ribs of the big wings were covered with nothing but cloth. The big letters under the picture announced:

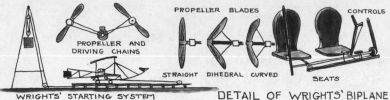

PROPELLER BLADES   CONTROLS

PROPELLER AND
DRIVING CHAINS

STRAIGHT   DIHEDRAL   CURVED

SEATS

WRIGHTS' STARTING SYSTEM   DETAIL OF WRIGHTS' BIPLANE

WRIGHT BROTHERS' AIRPLANE
PLANE FLOWN AT KITTY HAWK
NORTH CAROLINA 1908

"Think of it — 1908! Just two years ago!" exclaimed John Gray. "Seven years ago at this time, the first successful airplane hadn't even been invented!" Then he added mournfully, "Ninety-nine people out of a hundred haven't seen an airplane, and they won't see this one if it takes five thousand dollars."

"I'll tell you what, boys," said Sam White thoughtfully. Sam had a wise head on him, and the boys always listened when he began to talk. "Why can't we help out the men on the committee? Suppose we talk to every man we meet while we're delivering papers. Make every one see how important it is for Hastings to be the first city in the country to stage an airplane flight. Think of it! A real flying machine made by the Wright brothers! Make every man understand that he owes it to Hastings to donate some money!"

"Sure! We can do that!" shouted Charlie, all thrilled and ready to go.

Paper sacks were filled in the twinkling of an eye, and the boys were off.

"Hello!" called Charlie cheerfully to the first man he met as he turned the street corner. "Did you read the headlines? The committee can get an airplane for the Home-coming Celebration for only five thousand dollars. Everyone is going to help out. The committee is counting on you for some money, too."

The man happened to be Old Dan Cutter, and that was too bad for Charlie.

"What! What's this you say?" he exploded, his voice growing in astonishment and anger with every word he said. "Give me that paper! Who's counting on me? Who's counting on me for money?"

"Look out!" shouted Charlie, safeguarding his sack and sensing that he hadn't been very successful. "You can't have these papers! They belong to my customers!" And away he raced.

The boys did their best. Everyone was very much interested in the airplane, but *not* interested in giving money. Yet, by the time the last paper was delivered, most people understood clearly that the committee expected every man to do his duty.

Home-coming

"We'll have to raise the money now," said Mr. Lane in an amused tone. "Those boys haven't helped much, I'm afraid, but they meant well. We can't let them down after all this trouble."

"We won't," answered Mr. Hastings. "I'll call a meeting of my committee for tomorrow evening and plan some way out."

Every five years, on Labor Day, Hastings had a Home-coming Celebration. Each celebration was bigger and better than the one before. Of course, the Home-coming this summer must be the best of all. But after there have been balloon ascensions, and brass bands, and picnics, and parades, and a circus or two, it takes brains and imagination to think up something different. Fortunately, that is what Pinkie's father, chairman of the Home-coming Committee, had — brains and imagination.

"We must have a superattraction, gentlemen," he had said weeks ago, at the first committee meeting. Then he had come forward with a stupendous idea.

"We'll pack the trains coming into Hastings. We won't be able to take care of the crowds. First we'll go to Dayton, Ohio, to see the Wright brothers. We'll arrange with them to give a series of airplane flights in Hastings, the first flights in this state or even in this part of the country. I repeat, gentlemen, we'll pack the trains."

The idea had left the rest of the committee speechless but ready to act. And act they did. Now they were back from Dayton with good news and bad. The Wright brothers' agent would come, bringing with him two planes and pilots to fly them. He would come — provided he received five thousand dollars.

Fortunately, the chairman's imagination didn't end with one idea. At the committee meeting the next evening he had another. The mayor and the City Council sat around the table to hear the plan.

"This, gentlemen, is the plan," explained Mr. Hastings. "We'll stage the flights in the big Driving Park out on the Old Coach Road, an ideal setting for such an event. We'll charge fifty cents admission to the park, and every half dollar will go to make up the five thousand dollars. We'll raise money enough and to spare; but to be on the safe side, each one of you had better promise to donate a very little money in case we don't sell quite enough tickets. You'll never have to pay up. Of that, I'm certain."

Mr. Hastings certainly knew how to handle a committee. Of course, there were a few men who argued that since the big event was an airplane flight, all the people would stand outside the gate and look up instead of going inside and paying fifty cents. That would be just plain "horse sense." But there were others who insisted that the only people who would be outside the gates would be the ones who couldn't get in. So the argument went on; but before the meeting was over, one thing was certain. The Wright brothers' agent and the flying machine *were* coming to Hastings. There was no doubt about that.

Summertime is no time to sit around with your head in a book. If you are a boy and do that when fish are biting and the days are right for baseball, there must be some uncommon urge.

It *was* an uncommon urge which led Pinkie and Charlie, Jim Hastings and Sam, to spend a whole afternoon huddled over old newspapers and magazines at a table in the big Carnegie Library. If there was anything about the Wright brothers and their bicycle shop, about Kitty Hawk, North Carolina, and the first successful airplane flight on December 17, 1903, that the boys didn't find out, it was simply because it couldn't be found in that

library. That's all. And if, in the days that followed, crude models of flying machines, which the boys called gliders, appeared everywhere in Hastings, that was not surprising, either.

Now Pinkie was torn between two ideas of what he might do when he was a man. Should he make an automobile that could go a hundred miles an hour or an airplane which might even be able to carry another passenger beside the pilot, provided the passenger didn't weigh too much? Pinkie had discovered a few things in his experiments which he would like to talk over with Mr. Wright's agent when he saw him.

The date of the Home-coming was only a week away. The celebration was to begin with a parade and speeches on Saturday and continue through Labor Day on Monday. Each day there was to be an airplane flight.

The weather for weeks past had been intensely hot. Corn weather, the grownups called it, with the burning heat and the still, motionless air of a prairie summer! Late on Friday afternoon came a sharp electric storm, a sudden shower, and cooling breezes. Even the weather was to be ideal for the Home-coming. Surely nothing now could interfere with its complete success.

Wind Checks

On Saturday morning Pinkie was up with the dawn. Wasn't he to have a place in the Pierce Arrow, even if it was only on the running board? And wasn't it the Pierce Arrow which was to drive slowly about town with one of the airplanes hitched behind it so that all could see? Pinkie, scrubbed and shining and happy, was at the railroad station hours before the specially constructed baggage cars which were to bring the planes were supposed to arrive.

Trains coming into Hastings for days past had been thronged with people. Now wagons and surreys and buggies and carts jammed the roads into the city. By the time the train bringing the planes had arrived, the crowd was so great that Mr. Nickels, the Wright brothers' agent, refused even to think of unloading the planes for fear they would be broken to pieces.

Finally Mr. Hastings, standing high up on some soapboxes and talking through a megaphone, spoke to the crowd.

"Men, women, and children!" he called energetically. "Do you want to see the airplane flight planned for four-thirty this afternoon?"

"Yes!" thundered the crowd, as if with one voice.

"Then stand back!" ordered Mr. Hastings. "Until you do, the planes will remain in the baggage cars!"

The thoughtless but good-natured crowd, knowing that he meant business, fell back. One airplane was unloaded and hitched behind the Pierce Arrow. The baggage car with the other plane was shunted off on a sidetrack to the Driving Park to be put in condition for the flight.

Before many minutes the Pierce Arrow was moving slowly through the downtown streets with the brass band playing in front of it and the airplane following behind. A solid square of men had to form about the plane to protect it from a crowd which had never before seen an airplane and even now could not believe that this queer-looking machine with the cloth-covered ribs would ever leave the ground.

There was a cool, delightful tang in the air this Saturday morning. A brisk west wind was blowing, and the sun shone down from a cloudless sky. It would have been just as well if there had been no speeches. Everyone was too excited to listen.

By four o'clock the big grandstand at the

Driving Park was jammed with people. Hundreds overflowed onto the race track beyond, where the two planes, under careful guard, lay ready for flight. Eight thousand tickets already sold! So came the report from the ticket booth. And outside the gates another ten thousand people, unable to get inside the gates, waited with heads upturned to see an airplane actually rise into the sky.

Eighteen thousand people! Could any Homecoming Celebration ever again equal the success of this? Eighteen thousand people — waiting for the great moment and waiting in vain!

In a small enclosure close to the grandstand, a desperate committee was talking excitedly to Mr. Nickels.

"No use, gentlemen," Mr. Nickels was saying. "It's a bad situation, I agree. But the wind's too strong for a flight. I can't send a pilot up without endangering the crowd as well as the plane and the pilot. Better a disappointed crowd than a catastrophe!"

"We're in a tight place, Lane," said Mr. Hastings, and never before had he looked so worried. "If we give back the money now, as give it back we must, we'll never sell another ticket. Tomorrow the crowd *will* stand outside the gates."

"Why not give them a wind check?" suggested Mr. Lane. "A wind check instead of a rain check! The wind check will admit any person free on either of the other two days for which a flight has been planned." Evidently Pinkie's father was not the only man on the Home-coming Committee with brains and imagination.

The moment Mr. Hastings heard this, the look of relief on his face was wonderful to behold.

"You've saved the day," he said quietly.

But when he stood up before the grandstand, megaphone in hand, to proclaim the bad news, it was well that he belonged to the oldest family in Hastings, to the family which had done more for the city through the years than any other. It was well for him that most of the crowd knew him and believed in him. A certain note in his voice carried over to all who listened that his own disappointment was greater than theirs.

The crowd, for the most part, went good-naturedly away, wind checks in hand. "See you tomorrow!" many of them called jokingly to one another on the way out. "Be sure to keep the wind from blowing!" Only boys like Pinkie and Charlie couldn't joke. They were simply sick with disappointment.

The next morning it rained, a sharp downpour. Fortunately, by two o'clock the skies cleared. Again the crowd swarmed through the gates. In spite of the wind checks, a surprising number of tickets were sold at the ticket booth.

Shortly before four o'clock one of the planes was wheeled from under the awning which had protected it from the rain. The pilot began to tune up his motor. At last he was in his seat, perched away out in front of the two big wings.

Before the very eyes of the people of Hastings the airplane glided down the race-track runway! Before their very eyes that queer-looking flying machine actually left the ground — ten feet, twenty, forty, sixty! Up and up and up and on! The crowd, for a moment speechless with surprise, burst into a mighty cheer. Before the cheer was over, something went wrong. Down! The plane was swooping down! The pilot would be killed!

344

Another moment and the plane would fall on the watching crowd!

But fortunately the plane did not fall on the watching crowd. It landed in a cornfield on Mr. Derby's farm adjoining the Driving Park on the east. A lever had stuck and had caused the landing.

If the crowd, its fear instantly forgotten, vaulted the high fence about the park and spread through the cornfield, breaking down cornstalks as it went, it acted as all crowds act in the excitement of the moment. No doubt the plane would have been broken to pieces if the pilot, uninjured in the landing, had not sprung from his seat to protect it.

"Keep back! Keep back!" he shouted.

A runway was cleared through the broken-down cornstalks, and the pilot announced that he would attempt to fly the plane from the field. Cries of "Stand back! Give him room!" kept the surging crowd in check. But the attempt ended in failure. The plane caught in the corn and turned over, breaking five or six ribs as it turned. Finally it was righted and was wheeled ingloriously back onto the field.

Again a disappointed crowd left the Driving Park; and when on Monday, the last day of the celebration, it rained once more, Mr. Hastings wished that the idea of an airplane flight had never entered his head — *never!*

That night the *Evening Herald* carried cheering news. Hastings was still to see an airplane flight. Mr. Nickels promised on his honor that he would stay until snow flew if need be, until suitable weather would make the flight possible. Five blasts of the whistle in the Railroad Shop Yards would carry the news that the flight was on.

Tuesday morning people forgot their disappointment in the ordinary round of everyday work. After all, it was a question whether an airplane which could be depended upon to fly in all kinds of weather would ever be invented. Men weren't meant to fly and probably never would. Only boys like Pinkie and Charlie, back to school again after a long summer vacation, wouldn't work. Their ears were tuned to the sound of a shop whistle; and when school was out, they camped at the Driving Park every waking hour.

At ten o'clock on Thursday morning five long blasts announced the good news. If men poured from shops and factories, and housewives left their morning's work; if children thronged from school buildings and raced excitedly away; if everyone who could ride rode, and all those who couldn't ran to the big Driving Park, what else was to be expected?

Down the race-track runway went the plane, then up and up and up! One hundred, two hundred, four hundred — five hundred sixteen feet above the treetops! For almost an hour it sailed above the

city of Hastings while shop whistles blew and church bells rang, and people, looking up, stood speechless with the wonder of it.

Once again, in spite of difficulties, Hastings had "delivered the goods." After the gate receipts were counted, not one of the committee had to donate a penny. Even Mr. Derby's damaged cornfield was paid for; and if he didn't receive quite as much as he wanted, Mr. Hastings wasn't sorry. He remembered the tacks in the road.

Of all the people who watched the airplane flight, none felt the wonder of it more keenly than Banker Hastings. Safe from the push and surge of the crowd, he had stood beside the old-fashioned well curb of "The House on the Hill." Stood and looked upward! Perhaps the thoughts of a long-ago day, of a boy high up on the seat of a big brown stagecoach, flashed through his mind. Stagecoaches and covered wagons! Streetcars and railroad trains! Automobiles and airplanes, and the skyscrapers of a big city!

"In one lifetime," he murmured, "in my own!"

Even as he spoke, the crude airplane of the Wright brothers glided easily along above "The House on the Hill." What more could the future hold for Hastings?

TODAY — and then
TOMORROW

One Hundred Years of Growing

An early morning in 195–! High above the restless rumble of New York City was the bright blue sky of autumn. The deep hollows of the streets were dark with shadow, but the roofs and chimneys soaring far above shone sun-yellow in the keen, clear air.

353

Down the avenues and past the long, even rows of the cross streets, a big streamline automobile was humming its way. In the rear seat, their bags on the floor in front of them, sat a man and a boy of about ten.

Perhaps it was the crisp freshness of the air from the open window. Perhaps it was the pleasant anticipation of things about to happen. Whatever it was, there was something keen, alive, and eager about the way they sat and looked about them, something in tune with the push and hurry of the big city. The driver, weaving in and out with careless confidence in his own driving, glanced back with a reassuring nod as the big car whirred its way through the traffic.

"We'll make it yet, Tom, with even a minute or two to spare!" exclaimed the man confidently, looking at his watch.

"Make it! Of course we will! We'll be home in Hastings, eight hundred miles away, in time for lunch!" asserted the boy, with a quick show of spirit as he pulled an Airlines timetable from his pocket and examined it quickly. "Four hours and ten minutes, to be exact! I'll bet the whole family, Grandfather, too, is thinking of starting for the airport at this very minute!"

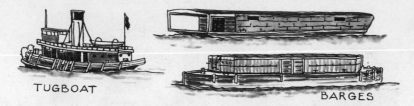

TUGBOAT

BARGES

Even as he spoke, the automobile was crossing a high bridge over a slow-moving river. The boy looked down upon a long line of empty freight barges, then gave a sudden jump of surprise as the lonely toot of a tugboat sounded beneath them. Minutes flew by, and the car was racing along a splendid parkway, then on and on again until it came to a great open stretch of land bordering a bay. Ahead of him Tom caught a glimpse of a low, wide-spreading building, mostly glass, with a glassed-in traffic control tower high up on the roof.

"Here at last!" he exclaimed eagerly, as the big car rolled quietly to a stop in front of the airport terminal.

Even as the porter came running for their bags, the man and the boy hurried into the ticket office, then paused a moment at one of the ticket counters along the wall.

"Hastings is the name! I reserved two tickets on the *Trail Blazer*," said Mr. Hastings.

"Flight Number 9! Here you are, and not a minute to spare!" answered the man behind the

ticket counter, tearing off half of each ticket and putting the other halves into an envelope which he passed across the counter.

Already the loud-speaker above the door of the waiting room was announcing,

"Flight Number 9! The *Trail Blazer* to Hastings now loading at Gate Number 3!"

"I've weighed your bags, sir. Both under forty pounds, and both O. K.," said the porter at their side. "They'll be waiting for you at the terminal when the flight is over."

A tip to the porter, and then without a word father and son hurried on their way. Another minute found them in a room with windows reaching from floor to ceiling, giving a clear view of a huge landing field just beyond.

Overhead two big liners were circling the airport in slow, wide circles, preparing to land. A huge plane was speeding down a mile-long runway, and still other planes were taxiing across the field to a stop at one or another of the main gates. From a hangar not far away came the putt, putt, putting

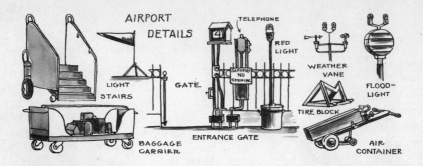

AIRPORT DETAILS

TELEPHONE

RED LIGHT

WEATHER VANE

FLOOD-LIGHT

LIGHT STAIRS

GATE

NO SMOKING

TIRE BLOCK

BAGGAGE CARRIER

ENTRANCE GATE

AIR CONTAINER

sound of a tractor pulling a huge flagship out onto the field.

"Attention, please! Flight Number 9! Nonstop to Hastings! Taking off in three minutes from Gate Number 3!" called the loud-speaker. "Passengers please go aboard!"

"Hurry, Father, hurry!" urged the boy, as they started down the long ramp which led from the waiting room to the gates at the edge of the landing field.

"Don't worry! We've still time!" Mr. Hastings started to say, when someone clapped him smartly on the shoulder and a voice, showing by its tone its owner's pleasure and surprise, exclaimed, "Pinkie Hastings, as I live! Where do you think you are going?"

For a second Mr. Hastings stopped dead in his tracks. "Charlie Lane, you old troublemaker!" he exclaimed, with a ring of pleasure and astonishment in his own voice. "I haven't laid eyes on you since the day you moved away from Hastings. I was hoping the centennial celebration would bring you back to town."

"Don't tell me this is another Tom," Mr. Lane continued, with a broad grin in Tom's direction. "Will that name never die out? Can it be that you're both boarding this plane for Hastings? I counted on seeing you when I got there, but I never hoped for the pleasure of flying home with you. Rare good fortune, I call it!"

As they were speaking, the men, with Tom in the lead, were walking up the gangplank, giving their names to the stewardess, and boarding the plane. Mr. Lane and Mr. Hastings, forgetting Tom in their pleasure at seeing each other again, chose a double seat on the right. Tom, content to be forgotten, sank down into the soft cushions of the single seat directly across the aisle.

It seemed as if they were no sooner in their seats than the cabin door was shut tight. From his window Tom could see men running out to remove the wooden blocks from under the wheels. One of the motors rumbled, turned over slowly, then let out a great roar, followed immediately by the second motor on the other wing. A red light appeared above the door to the cockpit; and as

a green sign, "Please fasten seat belts," flashed its warning, Tom hurried to fasten his belt for the take-off.

Tom and the other passengers were alive with interest, but Tom's father and Mr. Lane seemed scarcely to notice as the great plane rolled slowly away from the gate and taxied across the field to the runway. Once again, brakes set, the plane stopped while the copilot and the pilot received final orders by radiotelephone from the traffic tower.

Suddenly the propellers were whirling. The brakes were off. Slowly at first, then faster, faster, faster, faster, the *Trail Blazer* slipped down the mile-long runway directly into the wind. Another minute and the ground was falling away beneath, and the great plane was in the air, traveling the skyways to Hastings.

Higher and higher climbed the plane, one thousand, two thousand feet, and still higher, while the pilot swung the great nose gently about and headed to the westward. The roar of the motors died away to a humming sound. Within the cabin the everyday voices of men and women talked easily to one another, and down below New York City lay spread out like a great map with earth, sea, and sky in their loveliest colors.

For a time Tom sat staring from the window, almost too interested to unfasten his seat belt or to answer the questions of the stewardess, who asked how he was enjoying the ride. New York was soon left behind, and now down below were the greens and browns and yellows of harvested fields. Lakes shone blue through great stretches of woodland, and rivers wound like silver ribbons through the land. At times a large cloud would hide the earth beneath. At other times white-gray clouds floated by, bright with sun-dazzle. Everywhere were cities and towns and villages joined by long lines of highways along which cars like flies crawled endlessly.

The steady hum of the motors gave Tom a sleepy feeling. By this time most of the other passengers were reading or dozing in their comfortable seats. Then little by little Tom found himself listening to the interested voices of his father and Mr. Lane.

"So the old town is a hundred years old now, and the centennial celebration is tomorrow," Mr. Lane was saying. "Two hundred thousand people there now, you say? It doesn't seem possible!"

"Possible and true!" Mr. Hastings assured him. "Almost every day finds some new manufacturing plant building its factory or locating its main office there, or at least one of its branches. Now Hastings doesn't mean simply railroad shop yards, important as they may be. It means steel mills and tool works, road-building machinery and auto factories and harvesting machinery. It means elevated railroads and an airport and hundreds of other industrial undertakings."

"And your own airplane factory among them," Mr. Lane went on. "Whatever would our great-grandfathers have thought if they could have dreamed of all this?"

The men glanced up to find Tom standing silent beside them. A flash of understanding passed instantly between the men and the boy.

"Do you know what I see down there, Tom?" said his father after a moment, as he looked down from the window of the airplane. "I see the past down there, and a certain thing we call history.

"One autumn day a little over a hundred years ago, a big brown stagecoach was making its way along one of those long lines which was a road even in those days. High up on the seat with Lightning Joe, the driver, rode a boy, a Tom Hastings, too, and your great-grandfather."

"And while they were riding," continued Mr.

Lane, as if the next part of the tale belonged naturally to him, "they passed some covered wagons on their way west. A thin, long-legged, freckled-faced boy was driving one of the ox teams. That boy was Silas Lane, my grandfather. The first boy called to the second to tell him to be sure to stop in Hastings Mills on his way west."

"'Twas an important call, and one which made history," Mr. Hastings broke in to end the story. "The covered wagons did stop at Hastings Mills, and there they stayed. They found a few log cabins and your great-great-grandfather waiting for them. Then between them, the Lanes and the Hastings and a few other families began the building of a great city. You see how it all worked out, son."

Yes, Tom saw how it was. He had heard that story hundreds of times before and would hear it again with added interest. Today made it seem different. Now as he looked down from the window of the plane, he saw not only the greens and browns and yellows of harvested fields. He, too, saw the past down below there, the past and the thing called history.

Minutes flew by, minutes filled with the interested talk of two men and a boy.

Then suddenly the stewardess was passing along the aisle, announcing that the pilot was talking to the radio station in Hastings. The *Trail Blazer* was coming in.

"Fifty miles away! That's all!" she said smilingly to Tom. "Another fifteen minutes and you'll be safely home again."

"Look, son, we're beginning to coast down!" exclaimed his father, almost before the stewardess had finished speaking.

Sure enough, the great plane was dropping gradually out of the sky; and in the near distance, coming closer and ever closer, was the city of Hastings. How it spread out and how much of the earth it covered! Now it was directly beneath them with its tangled mass of streets, the railroad yards with long lines of freight cars, the river, the island, the great buildings with their roofs and chimneys clouded with the smoke from count-less chimneys. Only where the great city thinned out along the edges could be seen the red and gold of autumn trees, the green of grass, and the low-spreading homes of the suburbs.

Another minute and the tall office buildings of the city glided swiftly by, and ahead of him Tom could see the big airport. Lower and lower dropped the plane while again came the warning signal, "Please fasten seat belts." Now the pilot was circling the landing field in a great wide circle and talking by radiotelephone to the men in the traffic tower. The passengers yawned to clear their ears of the buzzing sound.

Down dropped the plane, lower and lower. The ground rushed up and glided swiftly by. The pilot throttled down the engines and dropped the brake flaps on the wings. Then gradually and gently he eased the great plane down onto the long run-way. Another minute and, with propellers whirl-ing, the plane taxied across the field to one of the main gates. And there behind the gate, waving and calling, Tom saw his grandfather, his sister Sally, and his brother Jim.

"Nonsense! No hotel for you, Charlie!" Mr. Hastings was saying. "You're coming home with me!"

A few minutes later found them all in a big streamline automobile on their way to the suburbs of the big city.

All the way home Jim and Sally chattered like magpies. All during lunch they could scarcely eat a bite. Even when Mother begged them to stop talking so someone else could get in a word edgewise, they still went on whispering excitedly to Tom. They couldn't help it. There was too much to tell.

"Wait until you see 'The House on the Hill'! Just wait! You've been away for weeks; and while you've been gone, it's been all fixed up. Just as it was when our great-great-grandmother lived there! All the things people have been collecting for years have been put in place ready for tomorrow. Spinning wheels and grandfather clocks and everything! Out in the carriage house are an old stagecoach and a covered wagon and even Grandfather's first Pierce Arrow car. Now don't you wish you had stayed at home!"

Tom didn't wish that he had stayed at home, but he did want to see. It was a good thing that Father and Mr. Lane were almost as eager as Tom. Lunch was no sooner over than back they piled into the car again, all except Mother.

Hastings was not reached in a hurry. The suburbs were too far away. But at last the car was rolling along through miles of paved streets bordered with big apartment buildings. On it went, through business districts where stores, hotels, and office buildings towered high on either side.

Now through the windshield Tom could see ahead of them a long hill sloping gently down into the valley of the Big Turtle River. On the hilltop to the right, huddled down behind its white picket fence in the deep hollow of the busy street, was "The House on the Hill." How small it looked, how low, and yet how friendly! Above the door, just beneath the patch of hand-shaven shingles, was the sign, "HASTINGS HISTORICAL MUSEUM, VISITORS WELCOME."

The car turned in at the carriage drive and rounded the low stone wall by the old-fashioned well. On it went beneath the two big maples which still shaded the wide stretches of grassy lawn. Then suddenly Grandfather, Father, and

Mr. Lane, Tom, Jim, and Sally were in the big hall
where the old-fashioned black-walnut stairway
curved gracefully upward. Old Martin, the care-
taker, who had been Grandfather's gardener for
years, was waiting to welcome them.

On the left of the hall was the parlor, almost as it had been in Tom's great-great-grandmother's day. There was a carpet with big red roses like the one which had covered the floor when the house was new. There were rosewood chairs and a slippery horsehair sofa, a marble-topped table and a whatnot in the corner. And on the walls was new wallpaper in an old-fashioned design, white with big gold roses.

For a long time the little group of people wandered at will upstairs and down through the old-fashioned rooms, out into the carriage house and barn and back again. Finally they found themselves once more in the old-fashioned parlor where the black-and-white portraits of Tom's great-great-grandmother and grandfather looked down upon them from the heavy gold frames on either side of the white-marble fireplace. Then suddenly Grandfather was talking.

"How interesting life is, and how it keeps on being interesting! When the first log cabin was built in the valley of the Big Turtle, this house, too, was a dream of the future. But tomorrow becomes today, and today slips into yesterday. Men live and things happen to them, and the ways of the world change."

"And that's history, isn't it, Grandfather?" said Tom softly.

"That's history," said Grandfather, "and your family and the families of other boys like you have a big part in its making."

As they turned to leave the house, the sound of their own footsteps followed them down the bare floor of the old hall. Outside was the bright blue sky of autumn, with soft, white clouds drifting slowly by and the sun going down over the valley of the Big Turtle.

"Paper, sir?" called a newsboy at the open window of the driver's seat, as the big car paused at the end of the carriage drive to nose its way into the traffic. "All about the big celebration tomorrow! It's going to be the biggest day in the history of Hastings!"

"Yes," thought Tom's father, as he dropped the money into the newsboy's outstretched hand. "History may be the record of life's yesterdays, but there is always the promise of tomorrow."

In this Glossary you will find the meanings and pronunciation of some of the words in *Engine Whistles*. Many of the words have more meanings than are given here, as you will learn by consulting your dictionary.

The pronunciation key will help you to understand what the diacritical marks mean.

The principal, or heavy, accent is indicated by the mark ′ after a syllable. In some words another syllable is also accented, but not so heavily. Such a syllable has the mark ′ after it—called a secondary accent.

The following system of indicating pronunciation is used by permission of the publishers of Webster's New International Dictionary, Second Edition, copyright, 1934, 1939, 1945, 1950, by G. & C. Merriam Co.

ā as in nāme	ĕ as in quiĕt	ŏŏ as in fŏŏt
ă as in văcation	ē as in ovēr	ou as in out
â as in dâre	ī as in mīne	oi as in oil
ă as in măn	ĭ as in ĭt	ū as in mūle
ȧ as in ȧccount	ĭ as in anĭmal	ů as in ůnite
ä as in färm	ō as in gō	û as in bûrn
ȧ as in ȧsk	ŏ as in ŏbey	ŭ as in bŭt
a̍ as in idea̍	ô as in ôr	ŭ as in circŭs
ē as in mē	ŏ as in nŏt	th as in then
ẹ as in hẹre	ô as in ôff	th as in thin
ê as in rêturn	ŏ as in fŏrget	t̶u̶ as in nat̶u̶re
ĕ as in gĕt	ŏŏ as in fŏŏd	

Glossary

a

ac com′pa ni ment (ȧ kŭm′pȧ nĭ mĕnt), that which goes along with or happens at the same time as something else.

ac cord′ (ȧ kôrd′), agreement in action or thought; choice.

ac cu′mu late (ȧ kū′mů lāt), to save up; to store up.

a cet′y lene (ȧ sĕt′ĭ lēn), a kind of gas made with water and carbide and used for lighting.

ac quaint′ance (ȧ kwān′tăns), someone you know.

ac′tu al ly (ăk′t̶u̶ ăl ĭ), really; truly.

af ford′ (ȧ fōrd′), to be able to pay; to be able to bear.

al′bum (ăl′bŭm), a book with blank pages, for pictures or for any other special records that one wants to keep.

an′gling (ăng′glĭng), fishing with a hook and line.

an noy′ance (ȧ noi′ăns), a feeling of being bothered or troubled.

an tic′i pa′tion (ăn tĭs′ĭ pā′shŭn), a looking forward to.

anx′ious (ăngk′shŭs), troubled or worried.

ap par′ent ly (ȧ păr′ĕnt lĭ), seemingly; appearing to be, but not necessarily so.

ar′bor (är′bĕr), a framework built for vines to grow over.

ar′ti cle (är′tĭ k'l), a written account of happenings, such as appears in newspapers and magazines.

as sert′ (ă sûrt′), to say as though sure of what one is talking about.

as sure′ (ă shŏŏr′), to say something to another person with the idea of making him believe what you say; to make certain.

at tire′ (ă tīr′), clothing.

at trac′tion (ă trăk′shŭn), something interesting that draws, or attracts, attention.

at tuned′ (ă tūnd′), in tune.

au′to graph (ô′tŏ grăf), one's own name in one's own handwriting.

a vail′a ble (à vāl′à b'l), at hand and suitable for use.

av′e nue (ăv′ĕ nū), a street, sometimes a wide, beautiful street.

b

ban dan′a (băn dăn′à), a large colored handkerchief with light spots or figures.

base′-burn′er (bās′bûr′nĕr), a heating stove in which coal is put in from the top and then drops, in amounts as needed, into the fire.

blast (blȧst), a loud, sharp blowing noise, as from a whistle.

brack′et (brăk′ĕt), a piece sticking out from a wall to hold a lamp.

bric′-a-brac′ (brĭk′à brăk′), small figures, dishes, and so on.

bri gade′ (brĭ gād′), a group of people working together on the same thing.

bril′liant (brĭl′yănt), very bright.

bro cad′ed (brŏ kād′ĕd), made from cloth with a raised pattern woven into it.

bur′ied (bĕr′ĭd), sunk; hidden; deep into something.

busi′ness (bĭz′nĕs), trade, or work.

c

ca′per (kā′pĕr), the act of leaping or dancing about.

car′bide (kär′bīd), a solid substance used in making acetylene gas.

car′bon (kär′bŏn), a substance found in coal, gas, wood, kerosene, and many other things, which, when burned, gives light and heat; a carbon lamp was one with a thread of carbon inside an airtight glass.

ca reen′ (kà rēn′), to tip or lean to one side.

ca tas′tro phe (kà tăs′trŏ fĕ), a sudden and very unfortunate happening, such as a bad accident.

cau′tion (kô′shŭn), to warn.

cer′e mo′ny (sĕr′ĕ mō′nĭ), a program carried out in accordance with plans made beforehand.

cir′cum stan′ces (sûr′kŭm stăn′sĕs), the facts at a given time.

com bine′ (kŏm bīn′), to join; to put together.

com mis′sion er (kŏ mĭsh′ŭn ēr), a person elected to do some special kind of public work, as a Highway Commissioner who looks after the building and upkeep of roads.

con fide′ (kŏn fīd′), to tell to another as a secret.

con′fi dence (kŏn′fĭ dĕns), a feeling of being sure of oneself.

con′fi dent ly (kŏn′fĭ dĕnt lĭ), with sureness; boldly.

con grat′u late (kŏn grăt′ů lāt), to tell someone that you like what he has done and are happy for him.

con′science (kŏn′shĕns) the sense that tells us whether we are doing right or wrong.

con′scious (kŏn′shŭs), knowing; awake to what is going on.

con′ster na′tion (kŏn′stĕr nā′shŭn), sudden fear or confusion.

con trap′tion (kŏn trăp′shŭn), an in-
vention.

cough (kŏf), to make sharp, sudden
noises, something like the gasping
sounds that come from your lungs
and throat when you cough from
a cold.

coun′cil (koun′sĭl), a group elected
to govern a town.

cous′in (kŭz′'n), the child of one's
aunt or uncle.

cro quet′ (krŏ kā′), a game played by
knocking wooden balls through a
series of wire hoops stuck into the
ground.

crotch′et y (krŏch′ĕ tĭ), having queer
ideas.

crude (krōōd), bare; not finished.

crust′y (krŭs′tĭ), cross.

cu′po la (kū′pŏ lȧ), a small, rounded
place built on top of a house, or a
roof that has been rounded.

cur′ry comb′ (kûr′ĭ kōm′), to clean a
horse with a currycomb, a comb
with rows of metal teeth or broken,
sawlike edges.

cush′ion (kŏŏsh′ŭn), a pillow.

cyl′in der (sĭl′ĭn dẽr), in an automobile motor, one of the hollow parts
with a rod inside that moves from
the force of the fuel.

d

dap′pled (dăp′'ld), spotted.

daugh′ter (dô′tẽr), a girl child.

debt (dĕt), money that one person or
group owes to another.

dec′la ra′tion (dĕk′lȧ rā′shŭn), a
statement or announcement.

def′i nite ly (dĕf′ĭ nĭt lĭ), clearly.

de′pot (dē′pō), a railroad station.

de scend′ (dĕ sĕnd′), to go down; to
sink.

de sert′ed (dĕ zûr′tĕd), empty; left
alone.

des′per ate (dĕs′pēr ĭt), wild; mad.

dis con′so late (dĭs kŏn′sŏ lĭt), very
sad.

dis′po si′tion (dĭs′pŏ zĭsh′ŭn), na-
ture; temper.

dis tin′guished (dĭs tĭng′gwĭsht), important or outstanding among
others.

dough′nut′ (dō′nŭt′), a small cake
made of fried dough, often shaped
like a thick ring.

dra mat′ic (drȧ măt′ĭk), with feeling
and expression.

e

ed′dies (ĕd′ĭz), round-and-round
movements of water.

ed′i tor in chief (ĕd′ĭ tẽr ĭn chēf), the
person at the head of a newspaper.

em bar′rass ment (ĕm băr′ȧs mĕnt),
a confused or uncomfortable feeling
that you have before other people
when you don't understand what
is going on or think that you may
have made a mistake.

em′bers (ĕm′bẽrz), smoldering pieces
of coal.

e mer′gen cy (ē mûr′jĕn sĭ), a situation that arises suddenly and that
has to be taken care of at once.

em′pha size (ĕm′fȧ sīz), to make
clearer and stronger.

en′er get′i cal ly (ĕn′ēr jĕt′ĭ kȧl ĭ),
forcefully; with spirit.

en tic′ing ly (ĕn tīs′ĭng lĭ), in a teasing, inviting way, such as to attract
attention.

---

nāme, văcation, dâre, măn, ăccount, färm, ȧsk, ideȧ, mē, hẹre, rĕturn, gĕt,
quiĕt, ovẽr, mīne, ĭt, anĭmal, gō, ŏbey, ôr, nŏt, ŏff, fŏrget, fōōd, fŏŏt, out,
oil, mūle, ūnite, bûrn, bŭt, circŭs, then, thin, natụre

ev′i dent ly (ĕv′ĭ dĕnt lĭ), clearly; plainly.

ex as′per at′ing (ĕg zăs′pĕr āt′ĭng), troublesome.

ex haust′ed (ĕg zôs′tĕd), worn out; very, very tired.

ex per′i ment (ĕks pĕr′ĭ mĕnt), to try out; to make a test; a t̂est.

ex tol′ (ĕks tōl′), to praise highly.

ex ult′ant ly (ĕg zŭl′tănt lĭ), in a delighted way.

f

fa mil′iar (fȧ mĭl′yẽr), well-known.

fas′ci nat′ed (făs′ĭ nāt′ĕd), strongly attracted.

fash′ion a ble (făsh′ŭn ȧ b'l), up to date; stylish.

fath′om (făth′ŭm), a measure of length amounting to six feet.

flare (flâr), to grow excited or angry suddenly.

flour′ish (flûr′ĭsh), a showy passage in music; a waving or swinging motion.

for′eign (fŏr′ĭn), from another country than one's own.

for′feit (fôr′fĭt), to lose something because of not living up to an agreement.

fu′ri ous (fū′rĭ ŭs), wild; raging.

g

gan′gly (găng′glĭ), skinny and awkward.

gauge (gāj), an instrument used to measure, or gauge, the size or force of something.

Gher′kin (gûr′kĭn), a humorous name for the funny fellow in the moving picture; a gherkin is a small cucumber used for pickling.

ghost (gōst), a spirit or a shadowy likeness; *the ghost of a smile* is almost a smile, but not quite.

gin′ger ly (jĭn′jẽr lĭ), very carefully and as if not liking what one is doing.

glo′ri ous (glō′rĭ ŭs), grand; splendid.

gra′cious (grā′shŭs), an exclamation meaning about the same as *Goodness!*

guf faw′ (gŭ fô′), a sudden, noisy laugh.

h

hal′ter (hôl′tẽr), a rope or strap with which to hold or lead a horse.

hand′ker chief (hăng′kẽr chĭf), a small square of cloth used to wipe one's face or nose.

haz′ard (hăz′ẽrd), danger.

ho ri′zon (hŏ rī′z'n), the place where sky and earth seem to meet.

i

im bed′ded (ĭm bĕd′ĕd), set in solidly; sunk.

in cred′i bly (ĭn krĕd′ĭ blĭ), in a way that is hard to believe.

in′de pend′ence (ĭn′dĕ pĕn′dĕns), freedom.

in′dig na′tion (ĭn′dĭg nā′shŭn), an angry feeling in a cause one thinks is just.

in dus′tri al (ĭn dŭs′trĭ ăl), having to do with trade or industry.

in fer′ (ĭn fûr′), to suggest.

in fer′no (ĭn fûr′nō), a very hot place.

in i′tial (ĭ nĭsh′ăl), the first letter of a name.

ink′ling (ĭngk′lĭng), the least little suggestion.

in tense′ (ĭn tĕns′), strong, deep, as an intense feeling.

in′ter spersed′ (ĭn′tẽr spûrst′), appearing here and there with other things.

in′ter vene′ (ĭn′tẽr vēn′), to come between.

i′rate (ī′rāt), angry.

i′sin glass′ (ī′zĭng glás′), a thin, strong, whitish substance that can be seen through.

j

jew's′-harp′ (jōōz′ härp′), a small musical instrument played by holding it between the teeth and striking a tongue-shaped metal piece with the finger.

k

knoll (nōl), a small, rounded hill.

l

lic′o rice (lĭk′ō rĭs), black candy made with juice from the root of a kind of herb.

m

ma'am (măm), a polite way of addressing a lady; it is a contraction of *madam*.

mag′pie (măg′pī), a noisy bird of the crow family.

mains (mānz), large pipes through which gas or water can flow from the main supply to the places where it will be used.

ma jes′ti cal ly (má jĕs′tĭ kăl ĭ), in a splendid or stately way.

man′u fac′ture (măn′ů făk′tůr), to make.

meas′ure (mĕzh′ẽr), to find out how much.

me chan′ic (mē kăn′ĭk), a person who knows how to build, run, and repair a machine.

Mer′ry Wid′ow hat (mĕr′ĭ wĭd′ō hăt), a large hat with plumes.

mis′er y (mĭz′ẽr ĭ), pain; suffering.

Mis′sis sip′pi (mĭs′ĭ sĭp′ĭ), a great river of the United States.

mo men′tum (mŏ mĕn′tŭm), the force of a moving body.

mos qui′to (mŭs kē′tō), a biting insect.

mourn′ful ly (mōrn′fŏŏl ĭ), sadly.

mys′ti fied (mĭs′tĭ fīd), confused; puzzled.

n

na′tion al (năsh′ŭn ăl), belonging to or coming under the laws of a country; in the United States, a national bank is one operating under laws set up by the government.

nec′es sar′y (nĕs′ĕ sĕr′ĭ), needed.

neph′ew (nĕf′ū), the son of one's sister or brother.

nick′el o′de on (nĭk′ĕl ō′dē ŭn), a moving-picture show that can be seen for a nickel.

nui′sance (nū′săns), a bother.

o

oc ca′sion (ŏ kā′zhŭn), a special event or happening.

oc ca′sion al (ŏ kā′zhŭn ăl), met with now and then; not often.

oc cur′ (ŏ kûr′), to come to one's mind.

of fi′cial (ŏ fĭsh′ăl), a person who holds public office.

o rig′i nal (ŏ rĭj′ĭ năl), first.

or nate′ (ôr nāt′), decorated; fancy.

p

pa′tient ly (pā′shĕnt lĭ), quietly.

pea′cock′ (pē′kŏk′), a large bird with very long, bright-colored tail feath-

---

nāme, văcation, dâre, măn, ăccount, färm, åsk, ideá, mē, hẽre, rĕturn, gĕt, quiĕt, ovẽr, mīne, ĭt, anĭmal, gō, ŏbey, ôr, nŏt, ŏff, fŏrget, fōōd, fŏŏt, out, oil, mūle, ūnite, bûrn, bŭt, circŭs, then, thin, natůre

ers that it can spread out in the shape of a fan.

peg'-top' skirt (pĕg'tŏp' skûrt), a long skirt that is narrow at the bottom and wide at the top.

per mis'sion (pĕr mĭsh'ŭn), leave for someone to do something.

per suade' (pĕr swād'), to win someone to your way of thinking.

pho'to graph (fō'tŏ grȧf), a picture taken with a camera.

plush (plŭsh), a kind of cloth somewhat like velvet, with a thick nap on one side.

pneu mat'ic (nū măt'ĭk), filled with air.

port'ly (pōrt'lĭ), rather fat.

pre dic'a ment (prē dĭk'ȧ mĕnt), an unpleasant situation.

pre fer' (prē fûr'), to like better.

pres'i dent (prĕz'ĭ dĕnt), the chief officer, or head, of a company.

pres'sure (prĕsh'ēr), force.

prim'ing (prīm'ĭng), pouring water down a pump to put it into working order.

prin'ci pal (prĭn'sĭ pȧl), most important; head.

pro ces'sion (prȯ sĕsh'ŭn), a group of people marching or riding along together.

pro pose' (prȯ pōz'), to offer; to have in mind.

pros'per (prŏs'pēr), to succeed.

pro vid'ed (prȯ vīd'ĕd), if; with the understanding.

q

quar'ter sawed' (kwôr'tēr sôd'), cut into quarters, as a log before boards are sawed from it.

r

re'al ize (rē'ȧl īz), to understand clearly.

re ceipts' (rē sētz'), money received.

rec'og nize (rĕk'ŏg nīz), to take notice of.

rec'ord (rĕk'ērd), an official writing down of facts.

re flec'tor (rē flĕk'tēr), a shiny or polished surface that acts as a mirror.

re lease' (rē lēs'), to let go.

re li'a bil'i ty (rē lī'ȧ bĭl'ĭ tĭ), trustworthiness.

re li'a ble (rē lī'ȧ b'l), trustworthy.

re tort' (rē tôrt'), to answer sharply; a holder in which substances are heated; a sharp answer.

rheu'ma tism (rōō'mȧ tĭz'm), a painful illness that affects the joints and muscles.

ri dic'u lous (rĭ dĭk'û lŭs), foolish; funny.

rough (rŭf), uneven; jarring.

ruch'ing (rōōsh'ĭng), a strip of fine, ruffled cloth or ribbon, used as trimming on the edge of a collar or cuff.

ru'in (rōō'ĭn), to spoil.

s

sat'is fac'tion (săt'ĭs făk'shŭn), contentment; the state of being satisfied.

scan'dal ized (skăn'dȧl īzd), greatly shocked.

scene (sēn), a view.

scoff (skŏf), to make fun of; to speak in a mocking way.

se'ries (sēr'ēz), a number of things in order, one after another.

se'ri ous (sēr'ĭ ŭs), thoughtful; grave; not gay.

shame'faced' (shām'fāst'), ashamed.

sheep'ish (shēp'ĭsh), embarrassed for having done the wrong thing; silly.

shied (shīd), turned or jumped aside suddenly.

si′dle (sī′d′l), to move along sidewise.

site (sīt), land set aside for a particular use.

sol′emn ly (sŏl′ĕm lĭ), with dignity; seriously.

sou′ve nir′ (sōō′vē nēr′), something to serve as a remembrance; a keepsake.

squab′ble (skwŏb′′l), a quarrel or disagreement.

stal′wart (stôl′wērt), big and strong.

suc′tion pump (sŭk′shŭn pŭmp), a pump that draws up water by sucking.

sul′try (sŭl′trĭ), hot.

su′mac (shōō′măk), a bush or small tree bearing flowers and berries.

sum′mons (sŭm′ŭnz), an order to appear at a certain place at a certain time.

su′per in tend′ (sū′pĕr ĭn tĕnd′), to oversee or direct; to boss.

su pe′ri or (sŭ pēr′ĭ ēr), proud; better than others.

sus pi′cion (sŭs pĭsh′ŭn), a pretty good idea; a misgiving.

sys′tem (sĭs′tĕm), an arrangement of separate parts that work together as a whole, as a water system.

t

tense (tĕns), keyed up; nervous; stiff.

teth′ered (tĕth′ērd), tied or bound.

thill (thĭl), one of the two long pieces of wood in front of a buggy or a wagon between which a horse is hitched.

thor′ough bred′ (thûr′ŏ brĕd′), a very fine animal.

tis′sue (tĭsh′ū), thin and fine, as tissue paper.

tres′tle (trĕs′′l), the open framework that holds up a bridge.

tri um′phant ly (trī ŭm′fănt lĭ), very proudly; joyfully.

trough (trŏf), a long, open box, not very deep, that holds water or food for animals.

twain (twān), an old word meaning *two*.

u

un′con cerned′ (ŭn′kŏn sûrnd′), indifferent, as if not caring one way or the other.

ut′ter ly (ŭt′ēr lĭ), completely; fully.

v

van′tage point (văn′tĭj point), a position in which one has an advantage, or the best chance to do what one has in mind.

vault (vôlt), to leap over.

vent′ed (vĕn′tĕd), let loose.

ve ran′da (vē răn′dȧ), an open porch, usually with a roof, along the side of a building.

vi′sion (vĭzh′ŭn) something imagined; a dream or a fancy.

w

whin′ny (hwĭn′ĭ), the gentle, neighing cry of a horse.

wreck (rĕk), an accident or a smashup to a train, ship, car, and so on.

wres′tle (rĕs′′l), a contest between two people, in which each person tries to throw or trip the other.

y

ye (yē), an old-fashioned word meaning *you*.

---

nāme, vȧcation, dâre, măn, ȧccount, färm, ȧsk, ideȧ, mē, hēre, rēturn, gĕt, quiĕt, ovēr, mīne, ĭt, anĭmal, gō, ŏbey, ôr, nŏt, ŏff, fŏrget, fōōd, fŏŏt, out, oil, mūle, ûnite, bûrn, bŭt, circŭs, then, thin, natṳre

Word List

The following list includes 1,042 words in this *Fifth Reader* that were not taught in the preceding books of THE ALICE AND JERRY BASIC READING PROGRAM. The word form or word combination here given is the one in which the word first appears. Since variants of these forms are treated in the *Teacher's Guidebook*, such variants are not counted as new words. Some sound words are not included in the list.

3–4

5 puffing
ripening
attuned
engine
curve

6 soot
cinders
smokestack
cab
sweat

7 burst
indignation

8 choo-choo
invented
Atlantic
admit
Stephenson

9

10 cord
deafening
blasts
twisting
efforts

11 clung
glimpse
critters
tender
grab

12 lot
throttle
Fourth-of-July
hissed
valve

13 glint
satisfaction

14 daisy
conscious
mayor
released
trestles

15 cane
bandana
scoffed
peering
job

16 swim
objects
specks
horizon
distance

17

18 sturdy
soil
prosper
spike
yonder

19 thousand
celebration
tank
glance

20 rate
fifteen
view
huddled

21 kerosene
lamps
brakeman

22 boomed
coupling
crash
slacked

23 charge
extended
gush
remarks

24 crew
president
coalbins
hose
pump

25 storage

26 exclaim
passenger
derby
gracious

27 doffed
sir
dirty
wipe
handkerchief

28 charms

29 wound
realized

30 Third
conviction
embarrassment
blood
mechanic

31 flare
guffaw
screens
plush

32 padlock
improve
soberly
polished
brass

33

34 yawning
Charleston
triumphantly
feller

35 main
semaphore
angles
beyond
parallel

36 block's
conductor

37 argument

38 apparently
motionless
tense
level
factory

39 depot
rung
balloon-shaped
slid

40

41 robin
woodpecker
marble-topped
curtains
carpet-covered

42 lace
picket
cousin
awhirl
principal

43 diving
starched
tying
scrubbed

44 budged
pitcher
soapsuds
gingerly

45 towel
bannister

46 basque
sleeves
ruffles
loose
tiny

47 mustache
Norah
petticoats
napkin
prisms

48 surrey

49 rheumatism
cuffs
nickel

50 attire
borders
ma'am
arbor

51 statue
lawn
shoo
vantage
tilt

52 squabble
Belle
buggy
stable

53

54 Avenue
deserted
outcropping
Cherry

55 phaetons
victoria
arching
currycombing
silver-mounted

56 halloed

57

58 twitching
DuSell
grove
truth
moment
59 dispositions
Mocking
Tray
attraction
business
60 verandas
small-paned
61 rambling
62 intense
present
Lincoln
vegetable
hollyhocks
63 initials
tooting
carpenters
64
65 pitching
wrestling
loafing
bustling
crazy
66 corncob
consternation
laughingstock
67 shanty
actually
fringe
parasol
plume
68 sash
satin
gloves
congratulate
extra
69
70 thrill
stamping
Broadway
71 false
hurrah
swung
uniforms
fifes
72
73 banner
platform
bedecked
74 gleamed
dignity
importance
cigar

75 struck
accord
sleek
carriage
Dinah
76 result
livery
barbershop
mortar
pestle
77
78 bottle
drugstore
jewelry
furniture
umbrella
79 Sawyer
hotel
rumbling
entrance
fleeting
80 bet
connected
perched
stuffed
guarded
81 grocery
82 sour
pickles
tissue
strips
licorice
83 fetch
hardware
cluttering
enormous
wedding
84 sparrows
eaves
flutter
planks
flourish
85 pace
dappled-gray
instant
sinking
86 flushed
resist
space
87 sheds
munching
available
oats
reserved
88 fancy
brocaded
gold-rimmed
89 Independence

90 beard
regret
future
thirty
midst
91 nudging
surged
sofa
92 grapevine
dents
scurrying
forty
93 seldom
swept
velvet
94 album
autograph
verses
bric-a-brac
wrecks
95 heaved
hay
haymow
hayfork
speed
96
97 priming
gurgle
sucking
nozzle
cistern
98 sizzling
pitting
cost
threaten
99 preferred
100 vaulting
101 newfangled
balance
102 series
intended
rough
club
nephew
103 Longshanks
chestnut
104 Prince
wobble
105 unconcerned
manner
dumb
inquired
106 retorted
brains
despair
procession

107 offer
desperate
manage
compass
108 fascinated
envy
victory
hesitated
109
110 visions
pedals
glorious
astraddle
rattle
111 equally
predicament
vented
112
113 conversation
confided
thoroughbred
114 guilty
nuzzling
whinnies
colt
ruin
115 pride
tingled
sunlit
weight
116 repeated
117 habit
greeted
groom
anger
118 nervously
nipped
shied
impulse
trough
119 raging
inferno
120
121 control
prancing
halter
flames
122 pent-up
flick
123 opposite
anxious
clang
volunteer
department
124
125 stalwart

126 brilliant
gauge
pressure
chips
127 district
128 suction
incredibly
combined
brigade
well-soaked
129
130 plus
terrific
exhausted
praise
bitterly
131 sunk
system
drilled
132 original
133 fact
Samuel
poppycock
exploded
good-natured
134 death
faucet
pure
135 lend
provided
bonds
cents
136 lent
funds
borrowed
fee
accumulate
137 vacant
taxes
property
expenses
138 election
voters
necessary
immediately
139 site
knoll
drown
140 Mail
sprawling
poking
Casey
policeman
141 law
obey
142
143 roaming
annoyance
confidently

144 tone
amount
prick
145 confidence
United
146 gig
clerk
sorting
packages
Express
147 rescued
blistering
midsummer
148 mosquitoes
149 examine
propped
buried
150 whack
professor
wart
graveyard
wicked
151 corpse
ye
Clemens
Twain
fathoms
152 Mississippi
153 funeral
discussion
154 recognized
coke
155 manufacture
till
156 jet
157 taper
charter
Council
operate
158 intention
159 spent
heaven
160 jew's-harp
161 pipestem
cheeks
embers
162 containers
slit
163
164 skedaddling
snoring
Huckleberry
Finn
widow
165
166 force
afford
167

168 dials
mystified
meter
169 brag
suspenders
Clancy
170 fifty
debts
divided
171 deal
risk
Ned
lecturing
172 stilts
fists
173 rag
bracket
reflector
brimful
superior
174 biscuits
lass
energetically
giggle
175 photograph
gallery
mournfully
176 red-and-green-
striped
chocolate
spied
177 nibbling
croquet
dreadful
178 exasperating
rumpus
winked
179 daughter
looped
ankle
pants
180 camera
standards
purple
haunches
fidgety
181
182 gangly
moaned
183 itched
darting
ordered
184 scandalized
rubber
bulb
gasped
relief

185 scene
madam
pleaded
186 disconsolate
absolutely
circumstances
completely
187 mantelshelf
glaring
justice
clattering
188
189 gradual
sumac
asters
hazel
thorn
190 capers
coaxed
sidled
crupper
191 buckled
bellyband
bridle
age
192 thills
slobbered
tugs
whippletrees
swallow
193 drawled
contraption
194 telephone
occur
suspense
tethered
195 consisted
196
197 urged
squirmed
braced
198 daze
Herald
create
sensation
199 thaw
dazzling
hushed
200
201 trudge
crannies
twilight
isinglass
base-burners

202 chapped
eddies
slashes
hub-deep
slush
203 furious
jam
sway
admiration
204
205 damage
affairs
flood
Capitol
206 grant
permission
forfeit
increase
spunk
207 generous
crisp
merged
sultry
208 pavement
solid
cedar
209
210 knocking
example
211 alert
superintended
212 James
213 gazing
murmured
214–216
217 weary
nicknamed
conscience
huge
218 proclaimed
elbows
sill
delivery
219 nags
clumsy
hobbled
spray
gong
220 steer
cylinder
lunger
balking
snorting
221
222 spurt
sprang
anticipation

223 closet
linen
visors
goggles
224 rigging
dignified
acquired
225
226 gasoline
convince
motorcar
brand-new
Model
227 automobile
228 Pierce
touring
229 reliability
pneumatic
folded
fenders
acetylene
230 padded
cushion
ruler
glory
231 suspicion
enticingly
harm
harsh
whooped
232
233 ridiculous
crank
gearshift
234 speedometer
235 jounced
gained
free
236 interspersed
heat-laden
237 rutty
bounced
occasional
238 Maxwell
punctures
five-gallon
emergency
exultantly
239 strain
240 sport
boasted
Park
soared
Peggy
241 unscrewed
flop
tack

242 smeared
cement
Dobbin
243 probably
244 cupola
simplicity
ornate
modern
grandeur
245 ceaseless
traffic
activity
suburbs
246 marvel
pleasure
Martin
Ellen
inkling
247 plate
cautioned
dining-room
Psyche
248 five-hundred-
pound
249 William
scissors-grinder
ding-dong
accompani-
ment
Tony
250 trolley
sputter
electric
collected
fares
251 oatmeal
extolling
merits
252 ruching
whalebone
distinguished
National
clever
253–254
255 nickelodeon
central
curb
notion
256 chisels
portly
definitely
Frank
serious
257 Rhodes
disturbed
swan

258 screamed
require
259 nuisance
Maggie
magniscope
magnifies
subject
260 booth
interior
261 crude
piano
punched
sheet
262 Ben
Gherkin
cure
263 grating
carbon
click
jerking
264 corkscrew
practically
mouse
265 spear
foil
266 crotchety
cape
peach-basket
film
267 custard
captured
broom
platter
Adeline
268 fraction
269 evidently
favorite
270 ivy-covered
drizzle
crusty
contrary
271 resolved
nerves
sipped
emphasize
272 ghost
porch
hoe
273
274 mar
strutting
peacocks
275 choke
bolted
reverse

Acknowledgments

The author of *Engine Whistles* is indebted to **Frederick L. Allen** from whose book *Only Yesterday*, published by Harper & Brothers, she used the idea, original with Mr. Allen, of describing the starting of a Model T Ford car in terms of clock time (see pages 274-275).

The black-and-white line drawings in this book are based on historical materials found by the artists in museums and in published works, some of which are still in copyright. The publishers wish to express their indebtedness to the following sources for copy adapted on the pages indicated:

Godey's Magazine, Harper's Bazaar, Harper's Weekly, and *Scribner's Magazine* between 1870 and 1880. Pages 7, 43, 46, 47, 50, 79, 94, 99, 122, 146, 155, 183, 250, and others.

The Franklin Institute of Pennsylvania. Pages 10, 22, 102, 127, 330, 331.

Romance of American Transportation by Franklin M. Reck, Thomas Y. Crowell Company, 1938. Pages 34, 35.

Growth of Industrial Art by Benjamin Butterworth. Published by Government Printing Office, 1892. Pages 67, 213.

A Manual of the Principal Instruments Used in American Engineering and Surveying, Manufactured by W. and L. E. Gurley, 1910. Pages 110, 306.

Enjine! Enjine! A Story of Fire Protection by Kenneth H. Dunshee. Published by H. V. Smith for the Home Insurance Company, 1939. Pages 122, 130, 131.

The Present Practice of Sinking and Boring Wells by Ernest Spon. Published by E. and F. N. Spon, London and New York, 1885. Page 139.

Turning Night into Day: The Story of Lighting by M. Ilin (pseud.). Published by J. B. Lippincott Company, 1936. Pages 155, 163.

Motor Magazine, Horseless Age, the *Automobile Trade Journal,* and automobile Catalogs between 1900 and 1910. Pages 223, 230, 231, 234, 242, 243, 244, 274, 275, 283, 286, 327.

Motion Picture Work by Hulfish, published by the American Technical Society, 1913, and *Magic Lantern Manual* by W. I. Chadwick, published by Warne, London, England, 1885. Page 267.

Safe Methods of Business written and published by J. L. Nichols, A. M., 1897, and *New American Business Guide* by E. T. Roe, published by John A. Hertal Company, 1926. Page 323.

Flying Machine by Rankin Kennedy, published by Van Nostrand, 1910, and *Vehicles of the Air* by Victor Longheed, published by Riley & Briton, 1911. Pages 330-331.